TUNNEL OF SECRETS

READ ALL THE MYSTERIES IN THE
HARDY BOYS ADVENTURES:

COMING SOON:

HARDY BOYS
ADVENTURES™

#10 *TUNNEL OF SECRETS*

FRANKLIN W. DIXON

ALADDIN New York London Toronto Sydney New Delhi

ALADDIN

An imprint of Simon & Schuster Children's Publishing Division

1230 Avenue of the Americas, New York, NY 10020

This Aladdin paperback edition October 2015

Text copyright © 2015 by Simon & Schuster, Inc.

Cover illustration copyright © 2015 by Kevin Keele

Also available in an Aladdin hardcover edition.

All rights reserved, including the right of reproduction in whole or in part in any form.

ALADDIN is a trademark of Simon & Schuster, Inc.,

and related logo is a registered trademark of Simon & Schuster, Inc.

THE HARDY BOYS MYSTERY STORIES, HARDY BOYS ADVENTURES,

and related logo are trademarks of Simon & Schuster, Inc.

For information about special discounts for bulk purchases, please contact Simon & Schuster Special Sales at 1-866-506-1949 or business@simonandschuster.com.

The Simon & Schuster Speakers Bureau can bring authors to your live event.

For more information or to book an event contact the Simon & Schuster Speakers Bureau at 1-866-248-3049 or visit our website at www.simonspeakers.com.

Cover designed by Karin Paprocki

Interior designed by Mike Rosamilia

The text of this book was set in Adobe Caslon Pro.

Manufactured in the United States of America 0915 OFF

2 4 6 8 10 9 7 5 3 1

Library of Congress Control Number 2015937423

ISBN 978-1-4814-3875-9 (hc)

ISBN 978-1-4814-3874-2 (pbk)

ISBN 978-1-4814-3876-6 (eBook)

CONTENTS

WHOLE

1

FRANK

M Y BROTHER JOE WAS ALREADY MORE than six feet underground when one of our hometown's most famous landmarks fell through a giant hole in the earth.

It was early Saturday afternoon. Just about all of Bayport had been planning to attend a street fair on the other side of town, but last week's disappearance of a couple of Bayport High School kids had put a stop to that. Instead most of the townspeople were gathered on the lawn of the square in front of city hall, waiting for Deputy Hixson to start a press conference. With our esteemed—and estimably grumpy—chief of police, Olaf, on vacation, the job of leading the investigation had fallen to his young protégé. But since Deputy Hixson's daughter, Layla, happened to be

1

one of the missing kids, he had a lot more at stake than just impressing his boss.

I felt bad for Deputy Hixson. He's a good cop. He's also a lot nicer than Chief Olaf when Joe and I interfere with a police investigation, which kind of happens a lot. As Bayport's foremost amateur detectives, Joe and I have a special knack for solving crimes. It isn't our fault that a couple of teenagers happen to be better at it than the local police.

We weren't officially looking into the missing kids, but Joe was friends with Layla, and I think he liked her as more than a friend, too, so we were keeping a close eye on things.

Joe wasn't at the press conference, though; he was under it! He was helping Urbex—the local urban explorers club—map some of the old tunnels hidden under Bayport, the same tunnels that we had helped discover on another case. Police press conferences were usually pretty dull, anyway, so we didn't think he'd be missing much.

But I wasn't just at the press conference to investigate. I was also there as a photographer. A camera can be one of a detective's most important tools, and I was intent on learning my way around my new digital SLR.

"Make sure to get some shots of Hixson's wife, too, Hardy," a sweet voice said not so sweetly behind me. "It would be great if you could get her crying while he's talking. The readers really eat up that emotional stuff."

I turned around to find Charlene Vale scribbling in the

little notebook she carried everywhere. Charlene was the news blogger for our high school's newspaper . . . and, to be honest, she was another reason I was at the press conference. She was supersmart *and* supercute and I kind of had a little—okay, maybe not so little—crush on her. She wasn't exactly warm and cuddly, though. Charlene took being an investigative reporter seriously, which I totally respected, even if it meant she was pretty intense sometimes. When I'd learned she was looking for a photojournalist to help document her stories, I joined the paper as a photographer.

"Once the press conference starts, I'll open up the aperture and use a longer lens. That will make the deputy in focus in the foreground with Delia slightly blurred behind him," I told her.

Charlene didn't look impressed. "I don't care if you draw a picture with crayons as long as you get the shot."

"Um, okay," I said, feeling myself blush. Sometimes I forget that not everybody gets as excited about technology as I do.

"Pretty big turnout," Charlene observed, thankfully changing the topic. "This disappearance is a big story. I'd love to be able to outscoop the *Bugle* on this one."

The *Bugle* was Bayport's daily newspaper, and it usually drew a lot more readers than our high school's student-run website. Not always, though. Charlene had already beaten the *Bugle* to the punch on a couple other big headlines this year.

And this *was* a big story. Hundreds of people had come

out to see what the deputy had to say—even some of the town's homeless population. I noticed a guy in his fifties, who everyone called Sal, pushing a shopping cart past the courthouse steps.

"You know, I tried to interview him once for a story on Bayport's homeless population," Charlene said, pointing to Sal. "He wrote 'no comment' on a piece of paper and walked away."

"I guess no one told you he was mute, huh?" I chuckled.

Sal had been a fixture around Bayport for as long as I could remember. I'd always wondered what his story was, but since he never spoke out loud, I'd never been able to ask him. I'd sometimes see him mouthing things excitedly, only no sound ever came out.

"I hear Delia Hixson is a member of the Mayflower Society," Charlene said as Sal pushed his cart past where Layla's mom was standing, waiting for her husband to address the crowd.

"Don't you have to be a descendant of one of the original pilgrims who sailed on the Mayflower to be a member of the Mayflower Society?" I asked. The history nerd in me got tingles. I hadn't realized any Bayport residents were related to some of the colonies' first settlers way back in 1620.

Charlene nodded. "I found out while I was doing background for this story. They've been Bayport bigwigs since Colonial times, living around here since before Bayport was Bayport. Longer than that guy even," she said, pointing over her shoulder to the large bronze statue of the Colonial navy officer that stood watch over the other end of the town square.

"You mean the Admiral?" I asked, taking in the statue of Admiral James T. Bryant, Revolutionary War hero of the seas and one of our town's foremost founding fathers.

"Did you know that Admiral Bryant's fleet of transatlantic merchant ships helped turn Bayport into a major commercial hub?" I went on. "He was friends with all kinds of important historical figures, like Thomas Jefferson and Ben Franklin. In fact, if things had gone differently, he might have made it into the history books too. He had big plans to turn Bayport into one of the nation's great port cities, but he disappeared before he had a chance. That's why Bayport stayed the sleepy little town it is today. The Admiral's disappearance is one of Bayport's great mysteries."

She gave me another unimpressed look. "If I ever do a story on the Admiral, I'll be sure to interview you."

Apparently I wasn't doing a good job impressing her with my knowledge of photographic technique *or* local history.

"Come to think of it, I can use Admiral Bryant's disappearance to draw parallels to what happened to Layla and Dan; it will give the story historical context," she said, nodding to herself and jotting the idea down in her pad. "See if you can get some shots with his statue in the background."

"You got it." I smiled. Score one for Frank Hardy!

"That statue really does kind of freak me out, though."

Charlene shuddered. "I keep thinking he's going to jump off the pedestal and start chasing me around with that giant fork of his."

It *was* a spooky statue. The angry-looking, twenty-foot-tall Admiral held a large trident in his right hand as if he were Poseidon, king of the sea. And if the trident—which actually did look a bit like a giant three-pronged fork—wasn't freaky enough, all you had to do was look at his other hand, which was missing its pinkie and ring fingers from a battle at sea.

But that wasn't the most interesting thing about his left hand. It was holding the coolest-looking book ever to his chest. The book was sealed with a clasp and engraved with all these strange symbols, like spirals, two-headed eagles, and an eye inside a floating pyramid similar to the one on the dollar bill. With his missing fingers and the way he was holding the book, it almost looked like the Admiral was giving the peace sign. There was also a giant bronze skeleton key dangling from a ring on his belt—the key to the city. What the trident and book symbolized, no one really knew for sure.

"According to legend, Admiral Bryant's ghost still haunts the old graveyard across town. It's just waiting for his body to be returned to the empty spot in his family tomb alongside his wife," I shared.

"The Admiral's Tomb, huh?" Charlene asked. "That doesn't make me feel any less freaked out by the statue."

I started thinking about the Admiral's mysterious disappearance as Deputy Hixson approached the microphone. The statue almost seemed to be watching the press conference from the other end of the square. It really did give the whole scene a sinister vibe.

"Thank you all for coming," Deputy Hixson said. I turned my attention, and my camera, back to the courthouse steps, where he was standing. "As you all know by now, two Bayport High students went missing last week: Councilman Saltz's son Daniel and my own daughter, Layla."

Deputy Hixson had to pause to collect himself. I could see the pain on his face, and my heart went out to him. I knew firsthand how hard it was to have to investigate a family member's disappearance.

"So far, we have been unable to establish a clear connection between the children. They are two grades apart in school, but they don't seem to have known each other. What we do know is that a suspicious figure in a hood was seen following both students shortly before their disappearances, and we have to consider the possibility that they were both taken against their will."

The crowd reacted with gasps and frightened murmurs.

"Please, everyone remain calm," Deputy Hixson continued. "I can assure you that the Bayport PD has devoted every available resource to finding them. We ask that you remain vigilant but calm and continue to go about your lives as normal."

As the deputy spoke, I could hear a rumbling sound in the

distance that I figured was probably just thunder. It wasn't until I felt a vibrating sensation in my feet that I realized the sound wasn't coming from the sky; it was coming from below.

"There is no, uh, need, uh . . . ," the deputy started to stammer midsentence.

As the rumbling grew more intense, people looked around in confusion.

". . . panic." Deputy Hixson had barely gotten the final word out when . . .

BOOM!

It felt like an earthquake and an explosion all at once. The ground rocked under our feet, and a huge cloud of dust erupted from the other end of the town square as the earth collapsed and swallowed the Admiral's statue whole.

BURIED ALIVE

2

JOE

"HEY, KEITH, DO YOU KNOW LAYLA HIXSON?" I asked.

The leader of Bayport's Urbex club just adjusted his headlamp, directing it toward the darkened tunnel branching off to our right. He grunted some sort of reply, but I couldn't tell if it was a yes or a no.

"Chris, Scott," he said to the two Urbex members who'd ventured underground with us, "you guys check out this passage. I'll take Joe down that way and we'll reconvene back here in twenty."

As far as I could tell, the tunnel we were exploring was right under the town square. A few months earlier, my brother Frank and I had discovered an old secret tunnel below the Bayport Aquarium that a wildlife smuggler had been using to steal an endangered giant sea turtle. We didn't know it then, but that tunnel turned out to be part of a whole network of abandoned secret passageways winding their way under Bayport. Some of them were hundreds of years old, but no one really knew who originally built them . . . or why.

Urbex had volunteered to help map the newly discovered tunnels. Keith and his team had a lot of experience exploring Bayport's abandoned structures and sewers, so they were pretty well qualified to safely lead the expedition. I wasn't an official Urbex member, but I knew Keith from rock-climbing class, so I'd decided to tag along at the last minute to get my mind off my friend Layla. It wasn't working, though.

"I'm usually pretty confident around girls, but Layla always makes me kind of tongue-tied, you know?" I shared with Keith, who ignored me as he led us deeper into the tunnel. "Maybe it's because her dad's a cop."

Keith started coughing like he'd gotten something stuck in his throat. It was pretty dusty in the tunnel, so I offered him a sip from my water bottle, but he just waved me off.

"Anyway, I finally worked up the guts to ask her out," I continued, "but she went missing before I had the chance! I can't help thinking if I had just asked her, maybe we would have been together the day she disappeared. Then I could have protected her from whatever happened."

Keith stopped without saying anything and began study-ing his hand-drawn schematics of the different tunnels. "I mean, at first, everyone was saying maybe she ran away, but that totally isn't like her. She's a genuinely happy person. And after Daniel went missing—I mean, come on, two kids from the same high school in one week?" I said, the detective in me starting to kick into gear. "You know the police have to be thinking it's kidnapping at this point, or they wouldn't have called a press conference on a Saturday."

Keith swung around abruptly so that his headlamp shone right into my eyes, making me see spots.

"Would you shut it already?" he snapped. "I'm trying to concentrate."

"Sorry, dude, just trying to make conversation," I said, raising my hand to block the light—not that it did much good.

"Well, don't," Keith muttered.

"Sheesh! No need to get all aggro about it," I said, wondering what had Keith so uptight.

He grunted. "Just stay here until I come back for you, okay? I'm going to check out that junction ahead."

"Fine, whatever, man," I said, trying not to get angry. I had invited myself on his expedition, after all. Keith had been pretty grumpy the whole morning, which was weird, because he usually joked a lot. I hadn't thought he'd mind me tagging along with the Urbex crew, but I was starting to get the impression that I wasn't welcome.

I watched Keith's headlamp grow smaller as he walked down the tunnel. Honestly, I wasn't thrilled about being left alone. It can be pretty easy to get lost underground if you're not careful. And the tunnels were spooky. Not that I was scared or anything. At least, not until a minute later, when Keith's light went out and he seemed to vanish into the darkness.

"Keith?" I called out. "You okay, man?"

There was no reply, and my headlamp wasn't powerful enough to see that far ahead. I tore off a strip of the neon-yellow reflective tape we all carried (the tape is easy to see when the light hits it), stuck it to a beam to mark my trail, and headed off down the tunnel. It ended at a T-section that split into two smaller tunnels. I shone my headlamp down one and then the other. Still no Keith.

I was about to call his name again when I felt the floor moving. A second later, a muffled thump sent a wave of vibrations through the tunnel.

I didn't know what was going on, but it definitely wasn't good. Before I had a chance to decide if I should go after Keith or run back to the rendezvous point, a *BOOM* rumbled through the tunnel, shaking the walls and knocking me off my feet.

There are two words you never want to have to worry about while exploring underground: *cave-in*. Judging by the chunks of dirt falling on my head, I was trapped in the middle of one! Instinct kicked in as the beam above me snapped. I rolled out of the way just in time to avoid being pinned to the floor. I slammed into the dirt wall where the tunnel split. My headlamp flickered, but it was still working. Not that I liked what I saw.

The path we'd come down was now totally blocked by rocks and debris, leaving me with two choices: left or right. I had no idea which way Keith had gone, but the tunnel on the left had less debris blocking it, so that's the one I took.

I pushed away all thoughts of being buried alive and kept my feet moving forward. Freezing up in a panic can be just as deadly as a falling beam.

I was focusing on taking slow breaths when I heard scraping and scratching. The sounds grew louder until I caught sight of the beam from a headlamp up ahead. Keith was on the ground, trying to clear away wreckage from another cave-in.

"Man, is it good to see you!" I cried. "What happened? Are you okay?"

Keith swiveled at the sound of my voice. He was covered in dirt and had a dazed look about him. "I'm, uh, okay. My ankle, it's sprained, I think. I, uh, we need to get out of here."

"I'm with you, man. I'll help you dig."

I quickly surveyed our situation. It looked like we were in some kind of underground chamber, only it was hard to tell because everything except the tunnel I'd come down was now walled off in rubble. It was mostly dirt and rock and some old beams, but then my headlamp flickered over something shinier on the ground.

I was about to move toward it when Keith started yelping,

"Forget about that! Why aren't you digging?! We have to get out of here now!"

He almost seemed on the verge of attacking me. I guess some people really can't stand being trapped in confined spaces. It seemed like an inconvenient phobia for the leader of an urban explorers club, but there was no time to think about that now. The two of us were trapped underground with a limited supply of air, and a wall of rubble between us and freedom.

3
LOST KEYS

FRANK

A S SOON AS WE SAW THE GROUND open up and swallow the Admiral's statue, Charlene and I sprinted across the town square. When I looked over my shoulder, I saw Deputy Hixson right behind us.

The air was so thick with dust that it was impossible to see anything. Deputy Hixson ran up behind me and put a protective hand on my shoulder.

"Stay back, Frank! It may not be safe."

"What do you think happened?" I asked.

"I have no idea," he said. "Some kind of sinkhole? I've never seen anything like it."

A crowd had started to gather, but the deputy kept everyone back until fire and emergency crews arrived.

It took a long time for the air to clear enough to actually see the giant hole in the ground where the Admiral's statue had stood and even longer to see inside the crater itself. The statue lay on its back fifteen or twenty feet below the surface amid piles of debris. Amazingly, the bronze statue seemed to still be in one piece. Well, almost; the oversize key that had been attached to the ring on the Admiral's belt was gone.

As I stared into the rubble-filled pit, I suddenly realized that the Admiral's key wasn't the only thing missing. So was Joe!

I'd been so distracted by what had just happened, I'd forgotten that Joe was somewhere under the town square exploring the old tunnels with the Urbex club. If he'd been anywhere nearby when the sinkhole collapsed, he could be trapped underground or . . . I didn't want to think about it.

"Deputy!" I yelled. "My brother and some other Urbex members were underground exploring when this happened. They're probably trapped!"

A man started shouting. "I think somebody's down there!"

"Everybody, quiet!" ordered Deputy Hixson.

CRRRRCK, CRRRRCK . . .

A sound almost like rocks scraping together echoed upward from the sinkhole.

"We're going to get you out!" I cupped my hands and yelled down. "Help is on the way!"

While the deputy organized and gathered tunneling gear,

a small boulder rolled away from a pile of wreckage at the sinkhole's bottom. A second later, Joe popped out. And he was carrying a giant two-and-a-half-foot-long bronze key.

Joe looked up at me with a big grin.

"Hey, bro," he said. "Anybody lose their keys?"

THEY KNOW!

4

JOE

THE LOOK ON FRANK'S FACE WHEN I emerged with the key was almost worth nearly being buried alive. It turns out that the shiny object I'd spotted lying in the debris had been the Admiral's missing key. The underground chamber Keith had been exploring was just a few yards from the sinkhole; he was seriously lucky the entire thing hadn't collapsed on top of him.

The bottom of the sinkhole was crazy, like a bombed-out crater where a twenty-foot bronze giant was a taking a nap. I quickly examined the Admiral's statue while the fire department hoisted Keith and me to the surface. Other than the lost key, the old guy looked none the worse for wear.

Frank reached out to pull me back onto solid ground. My

brother and I have this silent connection, sort of like twins (even though we're a year apart), and I could tell that he was as relieved to see me as I was to see him. My excitement faded when I remembered that Keith and I hadn't been the only explorers underground when the ground caved in.

"Chris and Scott are still down there," I told Deputy Hixson. "We have to go back to find them right now."

"Chris just texted me," Keith said hastily, waving his phone at the deputy. "They made it out through another entrance."

The deputy let out a huge sigh of relief. Then he took the heavy bronze key from me and examined it curiously.

"Lucky break everyone made it out okay," he murmured. "Just make sure to have the paramedics check you out before you leave."

"I'm fine, but I think Keith sprained his ankle pretty badly," I said. I looked around, but he was already limping away. He seemed pretty shaken up by the whole ordeal, and I couldn't really blame him for wanting to skedaddle as soon as possible. By the time the adrenaline rush from our close call had worn off, I was feeling a little shaky myself.

"Let's clear the square until we can ensure the tunnels haven't weakened the ground anywhere else," Deputy Hixson announced.

"Deputy, what makes you so sure the ground collapsed because of the tunnels?" Charlene asked, tapping the digital recorder she carried with her everywhere. "They've been there for hundreds of years, and this is the first time anything like this has ever happened."

Deputy Hixson looked skeptically at the recorder. "What else could it be? This is the first time people have explored many of them, so it probably just stirred up some of the old foundations."

"Can I quote you on that?" Charlene asked.

"What? No!" the deputy said with a frown.

"I don't know what things looked like from up here, but underground it sounded like a series of explosions," I offered.

"It seemed that way from aboveground, too," Frank agreed.

"That doesn't make a lick of sense," Deputy Hixson said.

"It's rare, but pockets of combustible gas can build up underground, although they usually need to be ignited in order to actually blow up," Frank said, going into Science Guy mode.

"Maybe the Admiral ate too many beans today," I suggested.

The deputy laughed so hard he snorted. He quickly tried to cover it up, clearing his throat. "It's probably just some sort of natural geological thing, like Frank said. We won't know more until the experts take a look. Until then, I don't want anyone else down in those tunnels."

The deputy shot Frank and me a hard stare that made it clear that last part was meant for us. He'd been around the Bayport PD long enough to know that we weren't always the best at listening when Chief Olaf told us not to do something.

"Anyone who ignores me on that is going straight to jail," he added before turning to Charlene. "That you can quote me on."

Deputy Hixson handed the big bronze key to another officer. "This broke off when the statue fell. Let's make sure it gets to whoever's going to be putting the big guy back together."

"You know what's weird?" I said. "It almost looked like the ring that was holding the key had been cut off the Admiral's belt with a blowtorch. It was a clean cut."

I took the key from the officer and pointed out the dark spot on the top of the skeleton key where it had been looped onto the ring. "And this burnishing looks a lot like torch marks," I pointed out.

The deputy waved his hand dismissively. "Probably just a weak point in the metal left over from that restoration a few years ago."

Sirens blared from across the square as emergency vehicles arrived.

"I've got to go. You kids stay away from that sinkhole," he reminded us sternly before marching off with the other officers.

They'd forgotten to take the key. I slipped it into my gear bag, hoping the Deputy wouldn't mind if we borrowed it for a while.

"All right, Hardy," Charlene said to my brother. "Show me what you got."

"Um, okay, sure," Frank replied not exactly confidently, turning around his camera and scrolling through the pictures he'd taken. Most of them were snapped before the press conference, with a few pictures of Deputy Hixson speaking. You could see the look on the deputy's face change as the ground started shaking. After that there wasn't much.

"I wasn't able to get the pic you wanted of Delia Hixson at the press conference because, well, the press conference didn't last very long," Frank said sheepishly.

"Yeah, but what about the sinkhole?" Charlene asked. "That's what everyone is going to want to see now."

"Well, I guess I was more concerned that everyone was okay. I wasn't really thinking about pictures," Frank explained.

"You can't print excuses, Hardy," she said. "There's some stuff here we can use in a pinch, but I want something that really grabs readers' eyeballs. Hit me up when you get that. In the meantime, I'm going to get some more quotes. Now I've got two front-page stories to file." She rushed off, recorder in hand.

Frank hadn't been joking when he'd told me Charlene took being a reporter seriously. Lois Lane Jr. was super intense. I could tell Frank was pretty crushed by her reaction to his pictures; I knew how much he wanted to impress her. But something else was bugging me. Something I'd seen in one of the photos.

"Can you flip back through some of those last pics?" I asked him.

"Why? They're obviously not very good," he complained.

"I'm not so sure about that," I said as he scrolled through the images. "Stop. There!"

It was a picture of Deputy Hixson conferring with the

mayor before the press conference. It wasn't them I was interested in, though; it was the woman in the background way off to the side.

"It's an okay picture, I guess, but there isn't much going on," Frank said.

"Can you zoom in on Layla's mom?" I asked.

"Mrs. Hixson? She's barely even in the picture. I—" Frank stopped short when he noticed the furious expression on her face. Even with big sunglasses hiding her eyes, you could tell she was *mad*. "It looks like she's arguing with someone out of frame."

"Do you have any wider shots so we can see who?" I asked.

Frank quickly scrolled through the images. "Nope, that's it. I took three or four pictures of the deputy and the mayor from the same angle. She's yelling at someone in each one, but that person is cut off."

"It might not mean anything, but I'd sure like to know what made her flip out at a press conference about her daughter's kidnapping. Could be relevant to the investigation," I said.

"Don't give up so easily," Frank said, smiling as he zoomed in even tighter on Mrs. Hixson's face. "Digital imaging has opened up all kinds of new forensic detection techniques. The resolution on this camera is high enough that I could enlarge the image enough for us to see the color of a person's eyes if I wanted."

"Yeah, but Mrs. Hixson is wearing sunglasses," I said, wondering what had Frank so smiley.

And then it hit me. We could probably see the person she was arguing with reflected in her sunglasses!

When I gazed at the image, I couldn't believe my eyes.

"Hey, is that—" Frank began.

"Sal?" I finished. There was no mistaking the raggedy homeless man's reflection. "Isn't he mute?"

"Yeah, but he communicates by writing things down. Look," Frank said, zooming in on the next picture. Sure enough, Sal was holding a piece of paper.

"Can you zoom in further?" I asked.

"That's the best I can do. The writing's too small and out of focus. But from the look on her face, whatever Sal wrote has her ready to flip her lid."

Frank scrolled to the next picture and zoomed in. This time Sal was scribbling something else on another sheet of paper, but all we could see was the back. Frank flipped to the final image and zoomed in.

"I don't know what Charlene was talking about, bro," I said. "Because that sure grabs my eyeballs."

Sal's face wore a terrified expression. The sheet of paper he held had just two words scrawled in large, shaky print:

THEY KNOW!

FAMILY SECRETS

5

FRANK

T HEY KNOW.'" I READ THE WORDS OUT loud. "Who knows what? And what in the world could Sal and Delia Hixson possibly have to do with each other? You don't think Layla's own mother could be connected to her daughter's kidnapping, do you?"

"I don't know, dude, but I see someone who might." Joe pointed to the street, where Delia Hixson was walking quickly toward her car.

We took off running across the square. Delia looked up in surprise when we caught up to her.

"Joe?" she said. "Can I help you with something?"

Joe got right to the point. "Mrs. Hixson, what were you arguing with Sal about before the press conference?" he asked.

Delia scrunched up her face like she'd suddenly smelled something awful. "I—I have no idea what you're talking about."

I clicked the shutter on my camera to get her attention. "I have pictures."

"And so will your husband if we have to submit them into evidence," Joe added.

Delia's shoulders sagged. "Please, no," she whispered. "I'll tell you about Sal, just let me be the one to tell him."

"Okay, we're listening," Joe said with a nod.

"Sal is my . . ." Delia's voice was barely above a whisper. "My uncle."

"What?!" Joe and I both blurted.

"How can that be? You're from an important family that helped found Bayport. Sal's a homeless guy who has silent conversations with himself." I stated the obvious, trying to make sense of it.

"He wasn't always that way," Delia said softly, sitting down on a bench by the street. "When I was growing up, Uncle Sal was the pride of the entire family. He was a gifted young engineer with a promising career ahead of him. But then something . . . changed."

Delia looked down at her hands as she spoke.

"He was working underground a lot for the city, something to do with the sewers, I think. He kept going on and on about some crazy legend having to do with a cursed treasure, claiming that our family was heir to a massive fortune buried somewhere below Bayport. I was a just kid back then and thought my uncle was telling exciting stories for fun. But the adults were worried. Soon even I could tell his behavior was getting more and more erratic. He was fired from his job because of it. It was a terrible scandal for the family. Father and Grandfather said he'd disgraced the Foreman name."

"Foreman? That's your maiden name?" I asked.

Delia nodded. "Uncle Sal would disappear for days and even weeks digging under Bayport. Then he would come home raving about the treasure, looking and smelling like a bum. Finally, on one of his 'expeditions,' as he called them, he was trapped inside a sewer pipe and . . . and he almost died."

Delia pulled a tissue from her purse and dabbed at her eyes.

"Uncle Sal recovered, but his vocal cords were so badly burned by the toxic gas fumes that doctors said he would never be able to speak again. The family tried to get him help, but he refused. He became so obsessed with his quest that he lost touch with reality altogether. He took to living on the streets. Our family was prominent in Bayport, and they . . . they disowned him. They simply pretended he didn't exist. It's become our family's darkest secret."

"Layla doesn't know she has a great-uncle?" Joe asked.

Delia shook her head. "My husband doesn't even know."

"How could you not tell the people you love about something so important?" Joe asked, unable to hide his astonishment.

Delia looked away again. "My family has been living this

lie for so long, I guess I started to really believe it. That he was just some crazy homeless man and not my uncle Sal."

She sat quietly for a moment before continuing.

"I didn't even think he remembered who I was until he approached me at the press conference. He was saying something ridiculous—that the Admiral's ghost kidnapped Layla to punish *him*, Sal, for meddling," she said.

"Admiral Bryant?" Joe asked.

"The guy whose statue just fell through a giant hole in the ground?" I added.

"Yes, strangely enough," she said, as if noticing the coincidence for the first time. "Sal wrote down that the Admiral's ghost was holding Layla prisoner in the 'Secret City.'"

I looked at Joe, but he just shrugged. "Never heard of it."

"Yes, well, apparently, it's the Admiral's underworld lair." Delia rolled her eyes. "Where he keeps his treasure."

"So let me get this straight. Your long-lost, crazy, and mute uncle comes to a press conference about your daughter's kidnapping to tell you that your daughter, his great-niece, is being held captive by the ghost of a famous Revolutionary War hero who died two hundred years ago," I recapped. "And you didn't think the police might want to know?"

Delia waved her hand in the air dismissively. "What good would it do? He's obviously delusional. The experience was very upsetting, but it was all gibberish."

"Yeah, but even if his story is nuts, just the fact that he's her great-uncle makes him a person of interest in the case," I told her. "He might know something for real."

"You're not just lying to your husband, you're withholding information from the police that could be relevant to your own daughter's kidnapping." Joe leveled with her.

"I would do anything to have my daughter back," she insisted.

"Everything except being honest with your husband," Joe mumbled under his breath. I put my hand on his arm to signal him to back off. We wanted to keep Delia talking, and making her more upset wasn't going to help.

"Sal wrote down the words 'They know.' What did he mean by that?" I questioned her.

"I asked him the same thing," Delia said. "He wrote that he had 'opened the vault.'"

She saw the confusion on our faces. "No use in trying to make sense of it. It's the ravings of a very disturbed mind. I don't know if he actually believes his own nonsense or if he was just trying to upset me, but I told him if he came anywhere near me or my family again, I would have him locked up in an asylum."

"Mrs. Hixson, I think it's time you told your husband everything you just told us," I said.

"But it could— But my marriage," she pleaded.

"Think about Layla," Joe said gently. "The police need to know everything having to do with her disappearance, even if it seems like a long shot. Your husband will be a lot more understanding if you come clean with him now than if you keep hiding something that could possibly help him find your daughter."

Delia nodded. "Thank you for letting me tell him myself."

"We have to check with the deputy later to make sure he knows," Joe said. "I hope you understand."

"Yes, thank you." She rose, then turned back to Joe.

"I don't blame you for being mad at me, Joe. You've been a good friend to Layla. When she comes home, well, if you wanted to ask her out, it would be okay with my husband and me."

"Oh, um, okay, thanks," Joe said, turning a shade or two pinker, which isn't something you see every day. I mean, I'm usually the one who does all the blushing when it comes to girls.

"Well, that's a new one," I said to Joe as she drove away. "I don't think we've ever had someone invite one of us to date their daughter during questioning."

"We have to find her first," he said.

"What do you make of Delia's story?" I asked.

"Which part? That Sal's secretly her uncle or that the Admiral's ghost is her daughter's kidnapper? It all sounds nuts."

"It's a crazy story, all right, but that doesn't mean her version of what happened isn't true," I said. "Though it's going to be tough to trust Delia knowing that she kept such a big secret from her own family. And even if she was telling the truth about Sal being her uncle, she could still be making up the story about the Admiral's ghost."

"We have no way of knowing for sure what Sal told her, or wrote her," Joe agreed. "And I don't want to burst my own bubble, but it's possible she mentioned me going out with Layla just to butter me up."

"It's awful to think about, but we have to at least consider the possibility that she knows more than she's letting on about her daughter's disappearance," I said.

"But why would she want to harm her own daughter?" Joe asked.

"I don't know," I said. "Who knows what other deep, dark family secrets she has to protect? She and Sal could even be in on it together."

"Or maybe he's blackmailing her," Joe suggested. "Sal being disowned by his family would give him a strong motive for trying to get back at them."

"From what I saw of the press conference, it's better than anything the police have to work with." It didn't sit well with me, though. Sal had always seemed so harmless. Some of the local kids made fun of him, but I always went out of my way to be nice when I saw him.

"Deputy Hixson will definitely want to interview him to find out where he was when Layla went missing," Joe said.

"As loony tunes as Sal's story sounds," I said, "don't you think it's a little strange that he warned Delia about the Admiral's ghost just a few minutes *before* the Admiral's statue was sucked underground by an inexplicable sinkhole?"

"Well, you know what Dad always says about coincidences," Joe reminded me. Our dad, Fenton Hardy, is a legendary retired detective who taught us a lot of what we know about investigating.

"It isn't coincidence when you make yourself look like a fool by ignoring a coincidence," I recited. "I don't have a clue how the Admiral and his ghost fit into it, but Dad also says that even the most far-fetched stories can loosen the thread that unravels the truth."

"Does that mean we get to interrogate a ghost?" Joe asked.

I laughed. "I don't know where to find his ghost, but maybe we can start by getting the lowdown on the real Admiral and his creepy statue."

"How are we going to do that?" Joe asked. "Did you find a time machine and forget to tell me about it?"

"Nope." I grinned. "The next best thing."

GHOST HUNTERS

6

JOE

I F THERE'S ANYWHERE IN BAYPORT WE'RE GOING to find pertinent information about Admiral James T. Bryant, it's here," Frank announced with an especially nerdy glow as we walked up to the information desk at the Bayport Historical Society library.

"Frank! It's good to see you again," said the bushy-haired man behind the desk.

"Hi, Mr. Schneider. We need to dig up some information on Admiral Bryant and his statue. There isn't much online besides the basics they taught us in middle school," Frank explained.

"I hear it's been an eventful day for the old Admiral," Mr. Schneider said.

"Not just the Admiral," Frank said. "Joe was underground exploring the old tunnels when the sinkhole caved in."

"Well, I'm certainly glad you made it out safely to join us, Joe," Mr. Schneider said.

"Yeah, I'm not so sure. Being trapped underground is a lot more exciting than being trapped in a library with my brainiac brother," I quipped. I quickly added, "No offense, Mr. Schneider."

Mr. Schneider responded with a good-natured laugh. "None taken, Joe, but maybe I can show you something that will make the library more exciting for you."

Now it was Frank's turn to laugh. "Fat chance. Joe won't read anything without pictures."

"Very funny, dude," I said. I may not be a hard-core nerd like my brother, but I do like reading. "I'd just rather read something more exciting than a history lesson about a crusty old dead guy."

Mr. Schneider gave me a sly smile. "What if that crusty old dead guy was caught up in rumors of ancient cults and marauding pirates?"

"Now that sounds like my kind of book," I said.

Mr. Schneider disappeared into the stacks and came back a few minutes later with a couple of old, leather-bound books.

"We're still in the process of digitizing our archives, so much of the information in our older volumes can only be gleaned through old-fashioned page turning. Or talking to me, of course." Mr. Schneider smiled proudly. "You already know the basic facts about our esteemed founding father,

Admiral James T. Bryant. Hero of the seas during the War for Independence and wealthy merchant mariner, whose grand plans and fleet of ships might have transformed our humble little town into one of the nation's great port cities were it not for his mysterious disappearance shortly after the town was incorporated."

"Don't forget the stories about him haunting the old graveyard," I inserted.

"Of course. It's a rather romantic story, actually," Mr. Schneider said. "The tomb he was supposed to share with the beloved wife who tragically passed away has two sarcophagi, but one is destined to remain empty forever. The lovers are never to be reunited—even in death."

I groaned. I wanted excitement, and instead the librarian was telling us froufy love stories.

"But that's all fairly common knowledge. What most of the local histories neglect to mention are the many legends and rumors the man inspired while he was still alive." Mr. Schneider opened one of the books to a yellowed page that had an old-timey illustration of a tall ship with raised sails and cannons.

It wasn't just any old ship either. This one flew an unmistakable black flag with a skull and crossbones.

"The local politics of the time were quite heated, and the Admiral had more than a few enemies," Mr. Schneider continued. "According to them, he wasn't a merchant at all, but a pirate king disguised as an honest businessman, who amassed his fortune by sending his ships out to plunder and pillage on the high seas."

"Cool!" I exclaimed.

"Really?" Frank asked. I knew what he was thinking—that maybe Sal's story about treasure had a hint of truth to it after all.

"None of it was likely true, of course, but at the time the newspapers had a field day," Mr. Schneider said.

Then the librarian flipped to a page filled with the same strange symbols engraved on the bronze book carried by the Admiral's statue.

"Other rumors, however, may have held more merit," he said.

Frank and I perked up. As far as we knew, those symbols were a total mystery. And the Hardy boys love a good mystery!

"You, no doubt, are familiar with the Freemasons?" Mr. Schneider asked.

"Sure! The Freemasons were a secret society that Colonial settlers brought to America in the seventeenth or eighteenth century, but no one really knows exactly where they came from originally," Frank chimed in. I just nodded, pretending like I knew what he was talking about. "The title Freemasons refers to the profession of masonry, or stone-work, and that's where the society gets a lot of its symbolism and rituals. Though some people say the order itself may have originated as far back as the ancient Druid or Egyptian

Isis-Osiris cults, other accounts say it started with the Knights Templar, the twelfth-century warrior monks who safeguarded the church's most secret treasures!"

Uh-oh! Frank had entered a full-on nerd warp! My brother gets super excited about this kind of historical stuff. He barely even paused to take a breath before going on.

"The American version of the Masons played an important role in early US politics. George Washington, Benjamin Franklin, and Paul Revere were all members. Some of the symbols found on US currency are supposedly inspired by freemasonry, like the 'Eye of Providence' on top of the pyramid on the dollar bill. The Masons have all kinds of secret symbols and rituals. A lot of people considered them a cult, but others claimed they were just a club of educated guys who got together to discuss intellectual matters. There are also all kinds of conspiracy theories about the Masons leading secretive underground movements throughout history— bent on world domination."

"So was the Admiral a Freemason?" I asked Mr. Schneider, knowing if I didn't cut in, Frank might never stop talking.

"He was, but that's not even the really interesting part," Mr. Schneider said. "The Masons spawned a number of smaller secret societies that are said to have ruled from behind the scenes throughout the Colonial era. While very little is known about the inner workings of Bayport's Masonic Society, its existence was widely known, and the

Admiral and his inner circle were assumed to form its core. So, along with defaming him by calling him a pirate, his political opponents also accused him of being an underground cultist with plans to control everyone in Bayport."

"Sounds like the Admiral was one rebellious dude," I said.

"Who knows how much of it was actually true, but it certainly made him a hot topic of conversation," Mr. Schneider said.

"And his affiliation with the secret society would explain all the cool symbols on the book his statue carries," Frank observed.

"The trident and the symbols that adorn the book undoubtedly held hidden meaning for the society, though sadly those details are mostly lost to history," Mr. Schneider said. "Unlike the Freemasons and a number of other early American secret societies that continued into modern times, the Admiral's little club appears to have disbanded shortly after his death. Local historians interpreted that as meaning he had been the society's leader."

"What about the key on the Admiral's belt? Do you know if that has any hidden meaning?" I asked.

Mr. Schneider gave me a curious look and hesitated a second before answering. "Not that I'm aware. I believe it simply represented the key to the city—a way to acknowledge his role in the town's early prosperity. Why do you ask?"

"Oh, no reason," I fibbed, thinking about the key hidden

safely in my gear bag. "Is there anything else you can tell us about the Admiral or the statue?"

The Admiral had turned out to be a lot more admirable than I had expected, but I wasn't sure what any of his rumored eighteenth-century exploits might have to do with the mysteries we were investigating.

"Not too much more to tell, unfortunately," Mr. Schneider said. "A lot of the local histories have been lost and his prominence beyond Bayport was cut short by his early demise, so he never made it into the national history books. We do know he was feared by a lot of people, but he was also uncommonly generous and was very charitable with Bayport's less fortunate citizens. He personally funded much of the town's early civic development, which probably accounts for the town erecting a statue in his honor while he was still alive and kicking. I'm not really sure what else you boys are looking for. . . ."

"Us either," Frank admitted.

"But there is one other book from that time that could shed a little more light. This way, gentlemen," he said as he stood up.

I lifted my gear bag (which was a lot heavier than normal thanks to the Admiral's key) onto my shoulder and followed Mr. Schneider toward the back of the library, where he pulled a very beat-up book from the stacks.

"Now, this came to us in very poor shape. It's missing more pages than not, but it does include some speculation about the Admiral's secret society from shortly after his demise."

Just then, a phone rang at the front of the library.

"If you'll excuse me, I need to get that," Mr. Schneider said. "Let me know if you have any other questions!"

"Thanks, Mr. S," Frank said as the librarian hurried off.

"I have to admit, if the history they taught at school was this interesting, I might actually pay more attention in class," I told Frank once we were alone in the stacks. "But . . ."

"It doesn't really help us understand what the Admiral or his statue has to do with Sal or Layla's disappearance." Frank finished my thought for me.

"Except that maybe Sal somehow learned about the pirate myth and took it a little too seriously," I added.

"Which doesn't make him any less crazy," Frank said.

"Nope." I dropped my bag in the aisle and started paging through the raggedy old book.

I stopped at an illustration of a figure in a long, hooded robe holding a trident a lot like the Admiral's. The figure had the face of a mouthless bird-man, with arched slits for eyes and a long crooked beak.

A tingle of fear shot through me as I read the caption aloud. "'Ghouls such as this have been glimpsed haunting Bayport's darkest alleys after the midnight hour. Were they summoned from the underworld as some suggest? Citizens are warned to venture out after sundown at their own peril.'"

"I guess people took things pretty seriously back then," Frank noted.

I flipped past a few more pages before I saw something else that made me stop. The page was partially torn, but the important part was still intact.

"Dude, you said Delia's family was big around Bayport way back in the Admiral's day, right?" I asked Frank.

"Yeah, they were supposedly one of the first families to settle the area. Why?"

I held the book open for him to read.

". . . others made public accusations that Bryant and his cronies were cultists. Among the more prominent citizens who came under suspicion were Mayor Samuel Smithwick, Treasurer Jedidiah Coleman, and Constable Joel Foreman."

Frank stopped reading. "Wait, isn't Foreman—?"

"Delia Hixson's maiden name? Yep," I affirmed.

"Do you think Delia and Layla could have been related to one of the Admiral's secret society brothers?" Frank asked.

"It would help explain why Sal is so obsessed with the Admiral," I said.

"It would also mean he isn't all-the-way crazy. There really could be a link connecting Layla and Admiral Bryant," Frank said.

"If there's truth to that, do you think there could be truth to his other statements? Like there being some kind of Secret City full of treasure?" I asked.

"I don't—" Frank stopped and looked up. "Hey, did you hear something?"

"Huh? Nah, dude, I—"

A second later a book fell off the shelf above me, conking me in the head. "What the . . . ?"

"Watch out!" Frank yelled, slamming into me just as the eight-foot-high bookshelf toppled over toward us.

Luckily, my brother had been paying closer attention than I had. Frank tackled me, pushing me out of the way just in time to save me from being crushed by an avalanche of books. Thanks to my brother's quick reflexes, neither of us were injured. When I looked up at him, he was staring past the fallen shelf with his mouth wide open.

"What just happened . . . ," I started to ask, but then I saw it too.

Standing at the end of the aisle was a red-robed figure with a monstrous beaked face and no mouth. Just like the one in the book we'd been reading.

Only this ghoul wasn't holding a trident. It was holding the gear bag where I'd stashed the Admiral's key!

Suddenly Sal's belief that he was being haunted by the Admiral's ghost seemed a lot less crazy. I was so stunned, I just sat there staring.

"It has the key!" Frank yelled, snapping me out of my daze.

The ghoul fled through the stacks, and we took off after him . . . or her, or whatever it was! The figure slipped through the back exit into the alley behind the historical society. We nearly lost track of it until I glimpsed its red robe up ahead.

"It's heading toward Central Station," I cried, pointing to the tall stone arches in front of Bayport's old train station.

The ghoul may have gotten the drop on us in the library, but we were faster, and the distance between us was shrinking. It ran into the station through a side door, and we sprinted in after it just a few seconds later.

There weren't many people in the big, open lobby, so the figure's red robe should have been easy to spot. Only it wasn't. The thief had vanished.

"Where'd he go?" I asked, skidding to a stop.

Frank looked around, stumped. "Maybe he slipped back out through a different door?"

"We should have seen him. Let's check behind the benches and in the restroom," I suggested.

The thief wasn't anywhere to be found. But someone else we were looking for was.

When we came out of the restroom, we spotted a scruffy, disheveled-looking man with a ratty duffel bag hurrying across the lobby toward a bunch of old luggage lockers.

"Is that Sal?" Frank asked.

"Sure is," I whispered, ducking behind one of the benches so he wouldn't see us. "Let's see what he's up to before approaching him."

Sal nervously looked around and headed straight for a shabby-looking locker with a sign on it that said OUT OF

ORDER. He glanced over his shoulder before opening the locker's door.

Frank and I spied from our hiding place, anxious to see what Sal was going to take out of the locker. Only he didn't take anything out. Instead he crawled inside and closed the door behind him!

"Huh?" we both said at the same time. I mean, it's not every day you see a homeless guy climb into a luggage locker. We shook off our surprise and ran across the lobby to yank the locker door open, but it was empty.

"Am I dreaming, or did we just chase a ghoul into a train station and then watch a homeless guy disappear into a locker like Houdini?" I asked Frank.

"That's it!" Frank exclaimed. "When Houdini disappeared, it was usually with the help of a well-disguised trapdoor."

I watched as Frank tapped along the sides and bottom of the tin locker. Finally he hit something that sounded hollow toward the back panel.

Frank was right. Behind the panel there was a hole with a ladder that stretched down into the pitch dark below.

This wasn't a locker. It was a gateway to the underworld.

THE MOLE PEOPLE

7

FRANK

UNFORTUNATELY, WHEN GHOUL-BOY took Joe's bag, he also got his headlamp, so we had to use the flashlights on our phones, which weren't superbright. By the time we'd shone them into the hole at the back of the locker, Sal was already long gone. "Here goes nothing," I said as Joe and I crawled inside, closed the door behind us, and began climbing down the ladder into darkness.

The ladder descended about a story before we hit the ground. The first thing I saw when we reached the bottom were train tracks.

"We must be in an old train tunnel under the station," I observed.

"From the looks of it, it hasn't been used for trains in a long time." Joe tapped on the dingy brick wall that sealed off the old tunnel from the station, then pointed his light down the tunnel in the opposite direction, where the track continued before vanishing around a bend. "I guess we're going that way."

"This tunnel must be from the old Central Station before they renovated it around the middle of last century," I said as we walked. "I remember reading about it. They kept the building because it was historically significant, but they put in a whole new track system. I guess they must have just sealed off some of the old ones and forgot about them."

"Man, the Urbex guys would get a huge rush out of this," Joe said. "How many people get to explore a place the rest of the world doesn't even know exists?"

"Delia said Sal spent a lot of time exploring under Bayport when he was still an engineer, so it makes sense he knew this was here," I noted as we approached the bend. "I wonder what else he discovered."

"I think we're about to find out," Joe said, pointing to the light that suddenly appeared at the end of the tunnel.

"That can't be fluorescent light, can it?" I asked as we got closer.

"That's what it looks like."

"That doesn't make any sense," I said. "There shouldn't be any working electricity down here. No one's used these tunnels for decades."

"Tell that to them," Joe said as we stepped out of the tunnel.

We were standing at the entrance to a large open space where a few different tracks converged, like a subterranean rail yard of some kind—only it had been entirely transformed into a bustling underground town!

The entire place was illuminated by modern lighting suspended from the ceiling. There were a bunch of people going about their daily business below. A guy I recognized as a local panhandler sat on a bench reading a newspaper, while a couple of scruffy old men played chess nearby. On the other side of the train platform a pair of young punks with multicolored Mohawks played with a dog, while a trio of women lounged in lawn chairs on a patch of artificial turf in front of an old train car. The "lawn" even had a white picket fence. More train cars stretched into the distance.

"This must have been the depot where they parked the trains," I speculated.

"Only the trains have been turned into condos!" Joe said, pointing at the lights in the windows and the shadows of people milling about inside.

"I've never seen anything like it," I replied. "Half the city's homeless population must live down here."

"I've heard of homeless people living in the abandoned subway tunnels under New York City," Joe said. "Urban explorers call them mole people. But who knew we had them right here in Bayport?!"

"Hey, we aren't moles!" a squeaky voice piped up.

We turned to see a scraggly bald man in a Christmas sweater poking an angry finger in our direction.

"And who are you calling homeless?" Another man in a well-worn secondhand suit said in a more friendly, albeit very deep and gravelly, voice. The man smiled and gestured at the train cars. "We have homes. You're looking at them."

"We didn't mean to offend you," I said. "We're actually really impressed!"

"Yeah, this place isn't mole-like at all," Joe added.

"We like it. It gives us a peaceful shelter from the cruel world above," Mr. Gravelly Voice said. "It can be hard for a guy to get a fair shake up there. People looking down at you, trying to deny you your rightful place in the world. Nope, civilization aboveground isn't always very civil to people like Curly and me, is it, Curly?"

"No sirree, Zeke. It's a hornet's nest of greedalistic oppressionalism, is what I always say," said squeaky-voiced Curly, whose hair may have very well been curly at one point, although there wasn't enough of it left to tell.

"How is it you boys managed to stumble upon our humble abode?" Zeke asked. "Not that I'm accusing you of hassling us, but we don't normally get many visitors down here."

"Actually, we were trying to find someone who might live down here. His name is Sal. Do you know him?" I asked.

"Hmm, let me think. Quiet, crazy type, right?" Zeke asked with a gravelly laugh. "Sure. Everyone knows Sal.

He's the one who built this place. Or at least the one who wired it for electricity."

"Sal did? Really?" Joe asked. "It's incredible that he did all this without anybody finding out about it."

I had to agree. Delia hadn't been lying about Sal being a gifted engineer.

"Yup. Guy's a certified genius. We even have working plumbing down here," Zeke said.

"And the Internet and six hundred thirty-seven channels of cable TV!" Curly chimed in.

"You don't mind me asking what it is you wanted with Sal, do you?" Zeke asked. "I don't mean to sound suspicious. It's just that Sal isn't exactly the socializing type. He can be a bit . . ."

"Certifiably bonkers?" Curly interjected.

"I was going to say 'unstable,' but that works too," Zeke continued. "Most folks down here are of the opinion that it's safer just to stay away from him, if you get my drift."

I didn't like it, but I got it. Sal might be dangerous. Which made it even more important that we find him.

"Actually, we have a mutual friend who is in trouble, and he may be able to help us find her," I said, cautious about revealing too much. Zeke seemed friendly, but it was never a good idea to give up information during an investigation.

"You must be talking about that missing Hixson girl. The one who's been all over the news?" Zeke must have seen the surprised look on our faces when he guessed right.

"Saw Sal walking around with one of the missing persons flyers the other day," Zeke explained. "It's a cruel world up there." He shook his head sympathetically. "I hope you find her."

"Do you know where Sal is now?" Joe asked hopefully.

"Nope, that's the last time I saw him. Sal can be a hard one to find if he doesn't want to be found. Just sorta comes and goes as he pleases. I don't mean to talk ill of the man after he's done so much for all of us down here, but he's not exactly the warm and cuddly type. Kinda creeps the rest of us out, if you want to know. No one really knows his story, and that makes people uncomfortable."

We did know his story, at least part of it, and it didn't make me any more comfortable. "You said Sal told you how to find this place?" Zeke eyed us suspiciously.

"Not exactly," I admitted sheepishly.

"We kind of followed him," Joe added.

"Huh," Zeke said, looking concerned. "Not like Sal to let himself be followed, but he's been a little more off than usual lately. Hey, Curly!" Zeke called out to his friend, who had wandered off to throw away an empty soda bottle. "You seen Sal?"

"Not today," called back Curly, who had started rooting around in the green recycling bin next to the trash can, pulling out pieces of garbage and tossing them into the black trash can next to it.

"People keep putting trash in with the recyclables," he

grumbled. "We may live underground, but we still have to worry about the environment up there. Take that earth-quake that swallowed up the Admiral this morning. My house shook so hard I thought it was going to jump right off the track."

Curly yanked another item of trash from the recycling bin, only this one wasn't trash at all. It was Joe's gear bag!

"Hey, that's mine!" Joe grabbed it from him and yanked it open. But I could already tell from how light it seemed that what he was looking for wasn't there.

"The key," Joe gasped. "It's gone!"

GHOST TRAIN 8

JOE

DID ANYONE SEE WHO THREW THIS OUT?"
I demanded.

Zeke shrugged.

"Wasn't me," Curly said. "I would have thrown it in the trash. Everyone knows this type of fabric isn't recyclable."

I locked eyes with my brother. There were only a couple of ways my bag could have made it from the ghoul's hands to this recycling bin: either the ghoul had used the same locker as Sal to make its getaway, or Sal and the ghoul were one and the same.

"Um, this may seem like a strange question, but you guys didn't happen to see someone in a red robe with, uh, a beak, did you?" Frank asked.

Curly gasped and dove behind the trash can.

"You mean the ghosts?" Zeke asked matter-of-factly. "Sure, people see them all the time." He wasn't joking. "I've never seen one personally, but you hear stories about the ghosts and ghouls that haunt these old tunnels. You said you saw one yourself, right, Curly?"

"Sure did," Curly said, peeking from behind the trash can. "Came right up and stole my sandwich when it thought I wasn't looking."

"Um, what do they do besides steal sandwiches?" I asked, not sure if I really wanted to know the answer.

"They're the Admiral's minions, of course," declared Curly. "They protect his treasure from thieves."

Frank and I stared at Curly, dumbfounded. Treasure? Sal had written about the Admiral's treasure when he and Delia had their argument before the press conference. Zeke leaned in to whisper, "Curly's a deck or two short, if you know what I mean. Folks think they see things sometimes, but it's mostly just imaginations running wild."

"You tell that to my sandwich!" Curly huffed.

I knew Frank was trying to process the same thing I was. Sal had said the Admiral's ghost kidnapped Layla and was holding her captive in the Secret City. It sounded crazy, but so did the fact that we were standing in the middle of an underground city conversing with a couple of mole people. Had we actually stumbled on the very place Sal was talking about?

"This place isn't called the Secret City, is it?" I asked.

"Well, technically, I guess it is a secret, although it might be a little generous to call it a city," Zeke said. "So, no."

Before I had a chance to get too bummed, Zeke offered a new ray of hope. "But I think I may know how to get to the place you boys are looking for. . . ."

This was it—the next big clue!

"Just follow the rainbow past Oz and hang a right at Hogwarts. You can't miss it."

Or not.

Zeke guffawed, clearly amused with himself. "I'm sorry, boys, I just couldn't help myself. Somebody's been pulling your leg. A mythical haunted city under Bayport? Preposterous! The place you're talking about isn't any realer than the ghosts who stole poor Curly's sandwich."

"It isn't a joke, Zeke," Curly said, turning to us. "It's where the Admiral keeps his treasure. Deep underground, a lot deeper than here, though no one knows exactly where— at least, no one who's alive to tell about it."

Curly looked over his shoulder and lowered his voice to a whisper. "The only ones who know how to find it are the ghosts that live there, and they make sure to keep it that way. Some say just speaking its name is enough to bring their curse down on you. Once that happens, well, they might let you live, but you'll wish they hadn't."

I gulped. I didn't actually believe in ghosts, of course, but down in those abandoned tunnels after the masked whatever-it-was had attacked us in the library and with Layla missing—well, it was enough to make even a level-headed guy like me want to start sleeping with a night-light.

"Take my advice," Curly warned. "Forget all about that place and go back up there where it's safe and sunny. You seem like nice boys, and I don't want to see you dead. Or worse."

Curly gave us a frightened look, then hurried back to his boxcar condo, slamming the door, bolting the lock, and shutting the blinds.

"Well, that's reassuring," I said.

"Scientifically speaking, there's no evidence to suggest that paranormal phenomena like the ones Curly described could even exist," Frank said, sounding less confident than I think he meant to.

Zeke just looked amused. "I wouldn't let Curly scare you boys too much. Like I said—it's preposterous! But . . . who knows? Maybe he's right. There are many tunnels and passageways running under Bayport. The ones that everyone aboveground has been all excited about lately aren't the half of it. Who knows what you'd see down there if you searched hard enough? Although I suspect all you'd find are cobwebs and sewer rats."

Whatever lay ahead, we had an obligation to Layla to investigate. So far all the crazy components of this case seemed to point back to one person, and I figured that person was a good place to start.

"Um, Zeke, if we did want to find Sal, where would we look?" I asked.

Zeke thought for a moment. "Well, I guess you could leave him a note."

"A note?" Frank asked.

"Sure. Sal's kind of like the maintenance guy around here, only he doesn't like talking to people, so he keeps a lockbox for folks to put requests when something needs to be fixed. Like running wires for a new resident or when HBO is on the fritz. Just take that tunnel to the junction and you'll see it on the wall."

Zeke pointed to a dark tunnel branching off from the open, well-lit space we were standing in. I unzipped my bag, took a quick inventory, and strapped on a headlamp. Luckily, the thief hadn't taken anything except the Admiral's key.

"Let's roll," I said to Frank.

"Thanks for your help, Zeke," Frank said.

"No worries. You boys keep an eye on your sandwiches," he said with a wink.

"Well, that was interesting," I said to Frank as we walked toward the mouth of the tunnel. "I don't think I've ever met anyone quite like Zeke and Curly before."

"I guess you have to be at least a little strange to choose to live underground," Frank replied.

I had an unsettled feeling as we entered the tunnel. I didn't love the idea of going even deeper underground in pursuit of someone everyone claimed was off his rocker, and walking into an enclosed train tunnel with barely any space between the track and the walls made me feel extra edgy. As we followed the track around a curve in the tunnel, my headlamp threw all kinds of ghostly shadows off the railroad ties in front of us.

"Is it normal to feel claustrophobic while urban exploring?" Frank asked meekly.

"Totally normal, bro," I said. "The important thing is to stay calm and it'll pass."

Frank sighed in relief. "Okay, that's good, thanks."

"No prob— Hey, what's that?" I asked my brother.

"What's what?" he started to ask, but then he felt it too. The tracks had started vibrating under our feet.

"That's weird," he said, listening to the low *clk-clk-clk-clk-clk* that followed. "It sounds kind of like a train, but that's not even possible. The cars down here have been out of commission for, like, a hundred years. It must be coming from the station aboveground."

"That's good. I'd like to avoid getting stuck in this tunnel with a train heading toward us," I said.

"Yeah," Frank agreed, laughing nervously.

"Um, Frank, what's that?" I asked again, this time pointing over our shoulders at a circle of light that had appeared on the track behind us—a light that was growing larger by the second.

Frank's eyes went wide.

"Train!" he yelled, and took off running like a rocket.

My stomach dropped.

"I thought you said it wasn't possible," I screamed, sprinting after him.

"Someone must have intentionally sent it down the track to run us over!" he cried.

"Unless it's haunted," I yelled back.

"Impossible!"

"You mean impossible like the train that's not supposed to be chasing us or a different kind of impossible?"

Frank ignored that one. "Whoever it is, they must not want us digging any deeper. That means we're on the right track."

"If this is the right track, I sure don't want to see the wrong one!" I said, trying to will my feet to go faster.

"Sorry, bad word choice!" Frank replied. The light behind us grew brighter, filling the tunnel and making our shadows dance along the tracks in front of us.

"We can't outrun it!" I yelled.

Frank screamed something else, but the sound of the train's wheels plowing over the track drowned it out. Then I saw it too—the wall with the lockbox Zeke had told us about—but that meant there was nowhere left to run! We were at the end of the line, boxed in with a brick wall in front of us and a train closing in from behind.

I sprinted as hard as I could for the wall, having no idea what we were going to do when we got there, but hoping it would at least give us a few more seconds to wish for a miracle.

I only had to pump my legs a couple more times before I saw that miracle. Or miracles. Two iron doors: one on either side of the tunnel. I went left and Frank went right. Mine was marked AUTHORIZED PERSONNEL ONLY. And it was locked.

Frank's didn't have a sign. What it did have was a huge skull and crossbones spray-painted in bloodred above the words STAY OUT—DEATH TO ALL WHO ENTER.

I didn't really care what it said. All I cared was whether or not it opened. And it did.

Frank threw the door open, but he hesitated before entering. Now wasn't the time for my brother to start worrying about curses.

The light from the train was blinding, the sound deafening. We were out of time.

I dove across the tunnel, plowing into Frank and shoving us both through the door a split second before the train would have plowed into us.

It didn't me take long to figure out why Frank had stopped, though. And it didn't have anything to do with pirates or curses. I'd pushed us straight off the ledge into a bottomless pit!

TICKET TO THE UNDERWORLD

9

FRANK

A SPLIT SECOND AFTER JOE SMASHED into me, the train smashed into the wall. A split second after that found us free-falling into a giant abyss behind the door I had opened.

Upon impact, the train exploded above us, spewing fire into the darkness and illuminating the vast cavern beneath us with an eerie glow. Giant stalactites like jagged teeth hung from the ceiling, and equally jagged rock formations and unstable boulders waited below. It would have been one of the coolest places I'd ever seen if I hadn't been witnessing it while plummeting through the air.

We weren't airborne long before we slammed onto a steep, rocky slope. There was just enough incline to break our fall, but not enough to stop us from tumbling the rest of the way down.

I clambered to get a handhold, finally grabbing on to a crag in the rock. Joe was about to slide right past me when I snagged his gear bag. One of the bag's handles tore free and the bag went flying, but it slowed him down enough to grab on as well.

"Whoa, dude," my brother said with a gasp, clinging to the rock beside me.

"I think I've had enough fun for one day," I moaned, trying to dodge the stones that had been dislodged by the exploding train and were rolling down the slope after us. "We'd better try to make our way to the bottom before the whole roof comes crashing down."

Joe surveyed the slope below. "There are plenty of natural handholds in the rock to keep us from sliding all the way down. Shouldn't be too bad as long as we go slowly."

As I watched Joe begin his descent, I heard a loud groaning noise coming from above.

"So you know what I said about going slowly?" Joe asked, looking up the slope past me.

"Yeah?"

"Well, new plan."

I followed his eyes up the slope, where a massive boulder was teetering from its perch. My stomach turned to ice as it began tumbling toward us.

"Slide!" he yelled.

He didn't have to tell me twice. I let go of the rock I was clinging to, and gravity and inertia took care of the rest. We shot down the slope like a couple of kids on a big, bumpy slide.

The boulder came careening down after us, smashing into the place we had been just a moment before and sending a landslide of smaller stones raining down on us. I could hear the boulder picking up speed, crashing into the rocky slope with enormous thuds that shook the whole cavern as it rolled closer, racing us to the bottom.

What we hadn't realized was that the slope didn't go all the way to the bottom. The end of it had crumbled away, leaving a vertical drop between us and the cavern floor!

My brother and I screamed as we fell off the edge.

The boulder, on the other hand, kept right on going, sailing over our heads close enough that I could feel it mess up my hair.

Joe and I crashed to the ground a few feet below, where we saw the boulder knock over giant stalagmites left and right like they were bowling pins before smashing right through the cavern wall.

"Oof," Joe said.

"Ungh," I replied.

"Are we still alive?" Joe asked.

"I think so," I muttered.

"What now?" Joe asked, picking up his gear bag from its landing spot nearby and dusting off his headlamp, which had also fallen off but was thankfully still working.

I craned my neck to look way, way up at the hole we'd fallen through. The flames from the train wreck had died to a flicker, making it look like a little yellow sun high up in the sky. The distance was enough to give me vertigo. If that slope hadn't been there to break our fall, we never would have survived the drop.

"Well, there's no way we're going back the way we came, that's for sure," I said.

"At least not without a couple jet packs," Joe said.

"So I guess we keep going. Lead the way, Cyclops," I told Joe, whose headlamp made him look like he had one big eyeball in the middle of his forehead.

Joe kicked aside a hunk of shattered rock as we followed the path of the boulder. "Man, those stalactites didn't stand a chance."

"Actually, the columns of calcium salt deposits that rise from the ground are technically called stalagmites," I corrected. "The ones hanging from the ceiling like icicles are stalactites."

Joe stopped suddenly. "Did you hear that?"

"What?" I asked, looking around nervously.

"The sound of my eyes rolling," he said.

"Ha-ha. You'll thank me when you take geology," I said.

Joe shone his light through the gaping hole the boulder had left in the cavern wall. "That's weird. It's like some kind of chamber."

"It looks like it was excavated by hand," I said, stepping

inside and running my hand over the wall. It was smoother than the naturally occurring rock on the other side.

Joe did a sweep of the room with his headlamp. The light filtered through the dust, landing on a splash of red. We climbed over a pile of rocks to get a closer look.

Staring back at us from behind a thick curtain of cobwebs were the hollow eyes of a partially mummified human corpse.

A corpse that just happened to be wearing the same kind of hooded red robe as the creep that had attacked us in the library. The robe hung in tatters over the dried flesh clinging to the mummy's skeleton.

"It looks like this guy shops for clothes at the same place as our ghoul." Joe shuddered. "As if dead bodies aren't freaky enough."

"Well, I guess we don't have to wonder about how he died," I said, pointing to the jewel-studded dagger sticking out of the mummy's back.

Joe winced. "Ouch. I wonder who he is."

"It's hard to even tell how old the body is," I said, trying to examine it without getting too close. "With this type of mummification, it could be fifty years old or two hundred and fifty. Or even older than that. The same conditions that allow the stalactites and stalagmites to form probably helped preserve him. Just the right mixture of minerals and mois- ture can suspend parts of the decomposition process. It's hard to tell more without doing a full forensic postmortem. You've got a pocketknife in your gear bag, right?"

Joe looked at me like I was crazy. "Leave the poor guy alone! He's already been stabbed once!"

"I'm not going to cut him open. I just want something I can use to lift back the robe without touching him."

Joe handed me a Swiss Army knife, and I unfolded the blade. As I reach forward to try to lift back the mummy's robe, I noticed something strange about the way its left hand was pressed to its mouth. It looked like the person had died trying to swallow something. But what really caught my eye were its mummified fingers. The mummy's left hand had only three of them. It was missing the pinkie and ring fingers.

Just like the Admiral.

"Joe," I said, "I think we just solved Bayport's oldest missing persons case."

DEADLY INDIGESTION

10

YOU MEAN THE DEAD GUY IS THE Admiral?!" I asked my brother.

Frank nodded, looking every bit as surprised as I felt.

"You mean like the-guy-in-the-statue-that-fell-through-a-giant-hole-in-the-ground-this-morning Admiral?" I asked again, trying to process it.

"That's the one," Frank said. "I'm pretty sure we just solved Bayport's coldest case. All the pieces fit. The rumors. The robe from the drawing in the book. The fact that he only has three fingers on his left hand."

I double-checked the mummy's fingers. Yup. Three. Just like the Admiral.

"I think we finally know what happened to Admiral James T. Bryant," Frank said.

"Not that it does him much good now," I said. "Or us, either, for that matter. We still don't know why he was down here or who killed him or, more importantly, what any of this has to do with the sinkhole or Layla."

Frank was stumped too. "Let's see if we can find anything on the Admiral's body that might give us more of a clue."

He carefully slid the Swiss Army blade under the collar of the Admiral's robe to pull it back. The problem was, the robe wasn't the only thing that pulled back. So did the Admiral's flesh!

An awful "MAAAAAH!" escaped from the Admiral's body, along with the two-hundred-year-old air that had been trapped inside, making it sound like he was groaning. We leaped back, Frank thrusting the blade in front of him like he was ready for a mummy attack.

Thankfully, the Admiral stayed where he was. His torso had split open like a dried-out turkey, though, so we could see all the way to his spine.

Frank laughed nervously and lowered the knife. "I guess his flesh stuck to the robe during the mummification process. It doesn't look like much of his soft tissue or organs were preserved, though."

I nervously rubbed my own stomach, feeling especially grateful that I still had one. And that's when I saw it. There was something lying at the bottom of the hollow cavity where the Admiral's stomach used to be.

"Hey, give me that," I said to Frank, grabbing the knife and opening the pliers. "I can't believe I'm about to do this."

I carefully reached inside the Admiral's corpse and lifted the object out with the pliers.

It was badly tarnished and corroded, but there was no doubt. It was an exact small-scale replica of the big bronze skeleton key that had been stolen from my bag.

I held it up for Frank.

"Whoa! It's a regular-size version of the key to the city that the Admiral has in the statue," he said. "He must have swallowed it before he died to keep whoever killed him from getting it."

"Talk about a last meal," I said.

"The gastric acid in his stomach wouldn't have been able to digest it, so it must have stayed inside him after his stomach decomposed," Frank informed me.

"Lucky break for us, though I'm getting indigestion just thinking about it." I groaned.

"I thought we might find a clue on his body," Frank said. "I wasn't expecting to find it *in* his body!"

"It must have been pretty important," I said, wrapping the key in a bandanna from my gear bag and sliding it inside my pants pocket next to the little emergency kit I carry when I go exploring.

"We're far below Bayport. It's not like he wound up here

by accident," Frank said. "I'm thinking this Secret City might be more than a myth after all."

"Yeah, well, judging from the knife in his back, that curse Curly was talking about might not be a myth either," I said.

"Just because the Secret City might exist doesn't mean it's haunted," Frank said. "We should try to find it as long as we're stuck down here."

"Too bad the Admiral didn't swallow a map along with the key," I said.

"I guess we just keep going," Frank said, stepping deeper into the chamber.

At the far end of the chamber, we found a narrow, partially concealed entrance into a larger corridor that branched off in two different directions. Like the chamber, the corridor had smooth walls, and I could see some of the chisel marks where it had been carved out of the rock by man-made tools.

"I say we go left," I said, thinking about the Admiral's left hand and the fingers he'd lost in battle. Not that we had much choice anyway. The passage on the right was caved in.

"Lead the way," Frank said.

It wasn't long before we stepped out of the passageway into a larger chamber with a shallow pond of clear water in the center of it. On the other side of the pond, high above the ground, was a perfectly rectangular opening. And dangling from the opening was the end of a rope ladder.

"I'm guessing that's not a naturally occurring rock formation," I said to my brother.

Frank took another look around the cavern and the sheer rock walls on either side. "Looks like the only way out; it's not like we can go back the way we came. There must be some kind of crank or pulley that raises and lowers the ladder. But how do we reach it? It's got to be at least three or four stories off the ground."

My headlamp threw shadows off a few dozen fist-size rocks that jutted out of the wall every few feet from the bottom to the top.

"It's a rock wall!"

"Thanks, Captain Obvious, I know it's made of rock, but how's that going to help us reach the ladder?" Frank asked.

For a supersmart guy, my brother can be pretty dense sometimes.

"No, like a rock-climbing wall. Someone intentionally carved all those stones into the wall as hand- and footholds so you can climb it. Like an ancient version of the rock walls at the gym. It's not even a very difficult one. I bet I can make it to the top in no time."

Frank gave me a concerned look. "You sure? We don't have any safety gear, and if you fall, well . . ."

He didn't have to say the rest. There were no ropes, harnesses, or partner on the wall to spot me. Without a system to keep me suspended, there'd be nothing to stop me from crashing to the ground. I was a pretty good climber, but I was still a newbie compared to the pros.

"I've got this," I said, trying to hide the nugget of doubt that had started to creep up on me.

We had to wade across the shallow pond to reach the wall. The water wasn't more than a foot or two deep, and I could clearly see small pebbles covering the bottom. Kicking aside the pebbles, I noticed symbols carved in the smooth stone beneath. There was a concentric circle and one that looked a little like a fishhook; I recognized them both from the cover of the book carried by the Admiral's statue.

"I hope we get a chance to tell Mr. Schneider about this," Frank said. "It basically proves that the secret society he told us about was real."

"Unless he already knows," I pointed out. "Maybe he's the one who attacked us in the library and stole the Admiral's key."

"Oh, yeah," Frank said gloomily. "It is convenient how the ghoul showed up in the library right after he walked away. Plus, he knows more about the Admiral's secret past than anybody."

"We'll worry about that if we ever make it back to the surface," I said, handing Frank my bag along with my backup flashlight.

I surveyed the wall before making my first move, mapping out the easiest route up the wall to the rope ladder. Whoever made it had built in a pretty straightforward path, with no more than a few feet between handholds. As long as I was careful, I would be fine.

I reached for the first handhold.

"Good luck," Frank said somberly.

"Who needs luck when you've got skills like mine?!" I said.

I started climbing, using my leg muscles to propel me from one handhold to the next, taking the burden off my arms like I'd been taught. It was a pretty easy climb, no harder than any of the walls at the gym. Still, I had to be cautious. I was high enough off the ground that I couldn't just hop off if my arms got tired. One little slip and I was a goner. I was feeling pretty confident, though.

Then I grabbed an unusual handhold. As soon as I put pressure on it, it tilted down about an inch, and I heard a strange metallic clicking sound.

Rock walls aren't supposed to make metallic clicking sounds. Not unless they're booby-trapped.

THE CAVERN OF DOOM

11

FRANK

I THINK I WAS MORE NERVOUS JUST WATCHING Joe climb than he was actually climbing. I was letting my brother risk his life, and I was pretty much helpless if anything went wrong.

Despite his confident act, I could tell he was scared. But I guess that's a good thing. I know from experience that a little bit of fear can sharpen your focus during life-or-death situations. Like our dad says, even heroes feel frightened sometimes; they just don't let it stop them from doing what needs to be done.

And Joe was handling it like a hero. Or a gecko. The way he was flying up the wall, you'd think he'd been born with sticky lizard feet. He was halfway up the wall and I was finally starting to relax when . . .

"Uh-oh," I heard him say.

"Joe, are you . . . ," I started to ask, when a whooshing sound cut me off. I barely had time to register the stone spike barreling down from the ceiling.

The wall was booby-trapped!

"WATCH OUT!" I yelled.

Joe let go with his right hand and swung away from the wall as the spike whistled past, leaving him hanging by his left hand. The spike shattered into a million pieces on the floor below, showering me with stone shrapnel.

I dove out of the way. When I looked back up, Joe was dangling from one handhold with both hands, struggling to regain his footing.

"Make sure to put your foot back on the same stone as before!" I yelled. "Any of the others could be booby-trapped too!"

It took an excruciating few seconds before Joe managed to steady himself.

"That was way too close," he called down. "So much for an easy climb."

"Stay where you are," I warned. "We have to assume the rest of them are rigged as well."

"Sure, I'll just hang here and read a comic book," Joe said sarcastically.

"Give me a second to think," I said.

Whoever had engineered this was serious about keeping people out (as if the Admiral's corpse hadn't been enough evidence of that). They'd made the climb look simple for a reason: Lure you in until you're too far up to drop safely and then—*wham!* Spikes start dropping, either skewering you like a kabob or plunging you to your death when you try to get out of the way. It was also possible that certain handholds had been rigged all the way up and Joe had just been lucky enough to avoid them. Either way, we had to figure out something quick, before his muscles gave out.

"I could try to follow the same path down that I took up," Joe called.

"It's too dangerous," I said. Even I knew that climbing down is a lot harder than climbing up. You can't see where you're going, for one. And Joe was already fatigued from the climb up, making his chances of falling a lot higher. I looked around the chamber, hoping something would spark a solution. There had to be a safe way up; how else would the people who'd built it reach the ladder? Either they'd memorized the correct path up—in which case we were out of luck—or there was a trick to figuring it out.

"Look," Joe said, "I don't mean to rush you or anything, but I'm getting a little tired up here."

"I'm thinking, I'm thinking," I said, trying to kick the problem-solving part of my brain into high gear.

"Couldn't they have left a map?" Joe lamented.

That was it! They *had* left us a map! I ran back into the shallow pond, kicking away the pebbles on the bottom, revealing the symbols etched in the stone.

"Now's not really the time to go for a swim, Frank!" Joe yelled.

"They *did* leave us a map, Joe!" I yelled back from the other side of the cavern, searching out a pattern in the symbols. If I was right, the concentric circles aligned with the path Joe had taken up the wall. The fishhook symbol represented the handhold Joe had grabbed when the spear fell. "The carvings on the floor of the pond aren't random. It's like a land-mine map, showing where the booby-trapped holds are and a safe path around them. I think I can use it to guide you up!"

"In that case, you'd better start guiding, 'cause I don't know how much longer my arms can hold out," he cried.

I took a deep breath and double-checked the patterns to make sure I was right.

"Okay, do you see the handhold above you to the left?"

"Yup, should I grab it?" Joe said, his hand at the ready.

"No! Not that one!" I yelled. "The one next to it. Do you think you can reach it?"

"I'll try," he said, stretching his hand as far as it would go and boosting off with his feet to make it the last few inches. For a terrifying moment he was totally suspended in air with nothing to hold on to. If he was short even a fraction of an inch, it was all over. I forced myself to keep my eyes open. And . . .

"Yes! You made it! Way to go, Joe!"

He made the next one too. And the one after that. And

the one after that. Pretty soon Joe was grabbing hold of the rope ladder and pulling himself into the opening.

My heart pounded and my forehead dripped with sweat . . . and I wasn't even the one doing the climbing! Joe lowered the rope to the ground using a crank that he'd found (as I'd speculated). I grabbed his gear bag and climbed up after him.

We were in the entryway of what appeared to be a long, dark corridor.

"Now that's what I call teamwork, bro," Joe said, throwing up a high five. "With your navigational abilities and my superior strength, coordination, bravery, good looks, and general awesomeness, the Hardy boys are invincible!"

He'd barely gotten the last word out when a heavy iron gate dropped from the ceiling with a loud clank, blocking the passage we'd worked so hard to reach. We pivoted back toward the ladder, but only made it a step before another gate dropped, sealing off the entrance as well.

And just like that, we were trapped. We'd climbed out of the cavern and right into a cage.

A flame appeared in the darkness. Two robed figures emerged carrying torches, light flickering over their inhuman faces and curved, birdlike beaks.

One of them carried an ornately carved wooden cane engraved with symbols. The other stepped silently to the bars of our cage and dropped a pair of heavy iron shackles at our feet.

From the looks of it, we had just become prisoners of the Admiral's ghost army.

THE SECRET CITY

12

JOE

"H EY, BIRDBEAK, YOU MIND LOOSENING these bracelets a little bit? I've got sensitive skin," I muttered as the ghouls marched us through a narrow, torch-lit passage. The ghoul with the cane used it to jab me in the back.

Both Frank and I were cuffed in wrist shackles that were linked to a single chain held by the non-cane-carrying creep; we were like a couple of dogs on a leash. I could tell Frank was deep in thought trying to figure out how we were going to get out of this. We'd tried talking to each other, but each time we got a sharp poke with the cane.

I'd been trying to keep track of where we were going, but the tunnels and chambers took so many twists and turns it was like walking through a maze. The explorer in me was pretty stoked, even if I was at the end of a chain led by a couple of cranky ghouls. At least, I assumed they were cranky; they hadn't uttered so much as a peep.

"No offense, but you guys are really bad tour guides," I said as we approached a crossroads where four different tunnels intersected. The one with the cane yanked us to a stop with the chain and gave me another jab in the ribs as he pushed past me.

I'll admit, for a second I had started to wonder if Curly had been right about the robed figures being ghosts. But as I watched the one with the cane step unevenly onto the crossroads to examine the symbols on the wall, I realized our captors weren't ghosts at all. Not unless one of those ghosts happened to have the same limp as a now-former friend of mine.

"Man, this place must be heaven for an Urbex pro like you, huh, Keith?"

The figure looked up. I was pretty sure Keith's mouth had just dropped wide open under his mask.

The ghoul holding the chain gasped. "They know who we are!"

"Shut up!" Keith yelled at his partner.

"Your name is Scott, right?" I asked Keith's flustered sidekick. "I'm guessing Chris is probably around here somewhere too."

"They know, Keith!" Scott said, his voice cracking behind his mask. I smiled. I'd guessed right about the other Urbex members being his accomplices.

"That's right, Scotty. And now it's all starting to make sense. You guys ditched me in the tunnel this morning on purpose. You planned to steal the big bronze dude's key out of the sinkhole until I found it first. Am I right, guys?"

"What are we going to do?" Scott said, panicking.

"I told you to shut up," Keith said. "It doesn't matter what they know. It's not like they'll get a chance to tell anyone. The Grandmaster will make sure of that."

I didn't like the sound of that.

"Um, Grandmaster?" Frank squeaked. Apparently he didn't either.

"So you don't know everything, huh? Well, we've got some surprises in store for you." Keith jabbed me in the ribs again, shoving us down one of the tunnels. "You like showing up uninvited, but this is one party you're going to wish you hadn't crashed."

"I'm enjoying it so far," I said, trying to hide the fact that I was scared witless. "This underground lair has to be one of the coolest things I've ever seen. How did you find it?"

"It's awesome, right?" Keith said, unable to hide his excitement. "This place is ancient. No one knows exactly who built it—early Native Americans, probably—but it was used as a hideout for pirates during Colonial times."

My tactic had worked. Keith was so caught up in the thrill of his discovery, he had dropped the tough-guy act. I knew Keith was a devoted urban explorer at heart and that he wouldn't be able to resist talking about it.

Scott wasn't so thrilled, though. "What are you doing, man?" he asked Keith. "That stuff is supposed to be a secret."

"Stop worrying so much," Keith said. "These guys won't see sunlight again unless the Grandmaster wants them to."

"So who's this Grandmaster guy, anyway?" Frank tried to sound casual, but the crack in his voice gave him away.

"He's the one who discovered this place. Or rediscovered it, really," Keith said. "This used to be run by Admiral Bryant himself. But after he vanished, it was forgotten. That is, until the Grandmaster reclaimed it for the Knights' descendants."

The Knights? I didn't know what he was talking about, but Frank seemed to be a step ahead of me on this one.

"The Knights were the Admiral's secret society, weren't they?"

Keith seemed surprised. "The Grandmaster is going to want to know how you found out about that, but yeah. The Secret Order of the Knights of the Bay."

"Keith, I really don't think you should be—" Scott began to protest, but Keith cut him off.

"If I want to know what you think, I'll ask."

Keith was playing right into our hands. I had a million questions, but I wasn't sure how much time we had before we reached where they were taking us. I wanted to know what had happened with the sinkhole and what this Grandmaster had to do with it.

"So what's the deal with stealing the Admiral's key anyway? You guys almost killed me twice trying to nab it."

"Yeah, sorry about that," Keith said, not sounding very sorry at all. "But your showing up at the last minute messed with our plans, so we had to ditch you. The tunnels weren't supposed to cave in like that. *Someone* put one of the explosives in the wrong place."

Keith whacked Scott on the back of the head.

"Ow! Jeez, Keith, I said I was sorry."

"Wait, so you guys created the sinkhole that swallowed the Admiral with a controlled demolition?" Frank said in disbelief. "That's like a crazy feat of engineering. If one thing went wrong, you could have brought down the entire square."

"Yeah, the Grandmaster is a genius. He designed the whole thing himself," Keith gushed. "He had the tunnels all mapped out and knew exactly where to set the charges. He could even identify the statue's weak points so I could cut off the key superfast. I would have been back here with it before the smoke cleared, but I got caved in and then you showed up again."

Keith couldn't resist giving me another jab with the cane.

"What can I say?" I said. "I have impeccable timing."

"I wouldn't be so sure about that," Keith said ominously. I could practically hear him smirking as he led us into an open space that looked like an underground coliseum carved out of stone.

Three balcony levels wound their way around the chamber's circular walls, looking down on a main amphitheater below. Each level was lined with stone dwellings of different sizes. Some of them had portals for windows and looked like they might be ancient dorms or apartments. Others had iron bars and looked like cells.

More masked figures had gathered around a creepy-looking altar at the center of the amphitheater. Behind the altar were steps leading to a large stone vault with a giant keyhole. The keyhole looked just the right size and shape for the Admiral's bronze key.

A large eye was engraved in gold over the vault, and something was written under it in another language. Frank took a moment to translate it.

"It's Latin," he whispered. "It means . . . Sacred Temple of the Secret Order of the Knights of the Bay."

"I think we found the Secret City," I murmured back.

"Tell the Grandmaster we apprehended two spies trying to infiltrate the city through the South Wall," Keith ordered the others, who immediately scattered.

"You!" He pointed to the shortest one in the group. "Come here. I need you to help escort the prisoners to their cell."

With Keith momentarily distracted and Scott busy trying to scratch his face under his mask, I saw our chance. I quickly made eye contact with my brother and gestured at the chain running from our shackles back to Scott's free hand. Frank got it right away, and we both yanked as hard as we could at the same time.

Scott yelped, falling onto his butt as the chain flew out of his hand. We took off running . . . which would have been a lot easier if we hadn't still been shackled together with a chain dragging behind us.

"Stop them!" Keith yelled.

We knocked over the short one, who had been standing frozen in place, and lowered our heads to bowl over another one like a two-headed running back. We might have made it too, if Keith hadn't managed to grab hold of one end of the chain. We tumbled into a heap on top of the ghoul in front of us and found ourselves staring at the end of Keith's cane—which now had a retractable blade sticking out of it.

Behind Keith, the short one we'd knocked over was still on the ground, fumbling to pick up a mask that had been knocked off in the scuffle, which allowed me a good look at its face. Or I guess I should say *her* face.

"Layla?"

THE WOMAN BEHIND THE MASK

13

FRANK

I LOOKED UP THE INSTANT I HEARD MY BROTHER say Layla's name. And there she was, like a kid caught with her hand in the cookie jar as she hurried to slide the mask over her face.

"Go to your room now!" Keith yanked her away by her robe, but the damage was done. She glanced quickly back at us before running off, but there was no way to read her expression beneath the mask. I had no problem reading my brother's expression, though: confused and betrayed.

Layla Hixson was one of them? Had she kidnapped herself? Had we risked our lives trying to save one of the bad guys?

I was trying to make sense of it as Scott and another one of Keith's masked lackeys led us up to a cell overlooking the altar.

The iron gate clanked shut, locking us in a dank stone cell barely large enough for two people. One of the walls had a small barred window into the empty cell next door.

Joe tested the gate's lock. "It's solid. I might be able to pick it if I had my tools, but they took my bag."

"At least they didn't search us," I said, motioning to Joe's pocket, where the small skeleton key remained safely hidden.

"Too bad it's not the right size for this lock," he said, sitting on the floor with his back to the wall. "Do you really think she's part of this? I know it looks bad, but I can't believe Layla would put her family through this."

"Her mom could be a part of it too," I reminded him. "For all we know, she, Sal, and Layla are in it together. Whatever *it* is."

Joe flung a pebble against the wall. Finding out that the girl you like might be part of a bizarre criminal conspiracy is a hard pill to swallow. We still didn't have all the facts, though, and the facts we did have didn't make a lot of sense. We'd managed to solve part of the mystery, but that just made it even more mysterious.

I started to review what we'd learned so far. "We know for sure the missing kids are connected to the sinkhole that swallowed the Admiral's statue, but we don't know how. We know how Keith and his accomplices caused the sinkhole and that they did it to steal the Admiral's key, but we don't know who's really behind it or what they need the key for. And we know it has something to do with the resurrection of an early American secret society started by Admiral Bryant, but we don't know why or what the master plan is."

"And we know we're locked in a cell a few hundred feet beneath Bayport, where no one will ever find us," Joe huffed.

"We've squeezed out of tighter spots than this." I tried to reassure him, but I had to rack my brain to see if it was true. Sure, we'd wrangled out of some tough situations before, but none as tough as this. The Admiral had spent about two hundred fifty years down here waiting for someone to find him!

Joe must have seen the doubt creep across my face, because he jumped to his feet.

"No, you're right. If Layla is innocent, we're going to help her. And if she's guilty, well, I'd hate it, but it's our job to prove it. Either way, we're going to make it out of here. After all, you've got a cute journalist to impress."

That was one of the great things about being partners with my brother. One would never let the other give up, no matter how dire the situation. It was a big reason why we *had* made it out of so many tight spots.

"Okay, we have to come up with a plan . . . ," I started to say, but I was interrupted by footsteps.

"Someone's coming," Joe hissed.

That someone was Layla.

She was still wearing her mask, but as the shortest of the cult members we'd seen, she was easy to recognize. Joe's eyes narrowed as she approached the cell door, carrying a tray of food and water.

She looked around.

"I'm not supposed to be talking to you. If they caught me, I could be in a lot of trouble, but I was able to convince the guard to take a break and let me bring your lunch. Or maybe it's dinner. It gets so confusing down here without any sunlight." Layla paused for a second and looked at Joe. "Did you really come all the way down here looking for me?"

Joe didn't answer. I could tell he was still figuring out whether she was the victim or the villain.

I nodded to Layla. "And we almost got killed a few times doing it, so I think you'd better tell us what's going on."

"Thank you guys so much," she said. There was no way to read her expression through her mask, but she sounded teary. "I didn't think anyone would ever find me."

"So you're not with them? Then why are you dressed up in that awful costume?" Joe asked, not bothering to hide his skepticism.

"They made me, I swear. You've got to believe me," she pleaded.

"Keep talking and we'll see," Joe said.

"Two of them grabbed me off the street after school. I think they drugged me, because at first I thought I was just having a bad nightmare, but I woke up down here. They told me there was no way to escape and that I'd die if I tried, so I went along with it until I could figure something out."

"Went along with what?" I asked.

"I don't know if you'll believe me. It all seems so crazy,

I don't even know if I believe it myself," she said.

"Try us," Joe said. "You'd be surprised what we'd believe at this point."

She took a deep breath. "Okay, well, these guys, the Knights of whatever they call themselves, they're supposed to be the direct descendants of an old secret society that was started by that Admiral guy from the statue in the town square."

I nodded.

"So this weird Grandmaster person is the boss, and he gives orders to that Keith creep and some of the others and they give orders to us. Keith said they were recruiting the other descendants to claim some kind of birthright. I told him kidnapping wasn't exactly recruiting, and he said that some people needed more convincing than others, but according to him, everyone came around and joined the club when they heard what they had to gain."

"Which is . . . ?" I prodded her.

"Pirate treasure!"

Joe and I exchanged glances. All the myths and legends Mr. Schneider had told us about in the library were turning out to be true.

"I know, it's wild!" Layla continued. "They say there are loads and loads of it. Enough for everybody to be superrich. I think it's a bunch of baloney, but who knows? I mean, this place exists, and I never would have believed that if you had told me before I was dragged here. And it does have a big vault. I guess anything's possible."

More pieces were starting to click into place. If the Knights thought the Admiral's treasure was locked in the vault and the vault wouldn't open without a giant skeleton key roughly the same size as the Admiral's "key to the city," well then, the theft of the key from the statue might finally make sense. And if they were targeting descendants of the original Knights, then Layla's kidnapping made sense too. That is, assuming Sal was right and they were related to the Constable Foreman from the old book Mr. Schneider showed us.

I was tempted to interrupt with questions, but Layla was on a roll.

"But what do I need a treasure for? I'm in high school! And my dad's practically the sheriff. Like I'd really go behind his back and be a part of some crazy conspiracy. I'd be grounded until I was thirty!" Layla looked around nervously and lowered her voice. "But that's why they wanted me so badly—because my dad *is* deputy sheriff. They say they're going to use the treasure to fund some master plan to take control of all of Bayport. They want me to follow in my dad's footsteps and rise through the police force so that they can have a Knight to pull strings from inside the department. Nuts, right?"

I nodded, encouraging her to keep talking.

"They say they already have other important people in the mayor's office, as well as the kid of a city councilman."

"Is it Daniel Saltz?" I asked. "Councilman Saltz's son?"

"That would explain the other kidnapped student," Joe

commented. "He must be related to one of the original Knights too."

Layla shrugged. "I don't know who it is, because they make everyone wear masks all the time except when we're alone in our rooms. People gossip when Keith isn't around, but I don't recognize their voices, and they all seem totally on board with the plan anyway, so I just keep my mouth shut. You guys are the first people I've talked to in a week! I'm totally rambling, aren't I? You don't how good it feels to finally be able to tell somebody all this!"

From his face, I knew Joe was struggling with whether or not to believe her. I was distracted by something else, though.

"Um, are those Hot Pockets?" I asked, noticing the contents of the tray she'd been carrying.

"Yeah, that's about all we eat down here. Hot Pockets, pizza rolls, and instant popcorn. It's totally killing my diet."

"But we're in an ancient underground city halfway to the center of the earth. Do you cook them over hot coals or something?" Joe asked.

"Nah, we use the microwave," she said nonchalantly.

She must have seen the surprise on our faces.

"Oh yeah, they totally have electricity down here. The whole place is wired. All those torches are just for theatrics, as far as I can tell. There's actually a full kitchen and a game room with a fifty-inch flat-screen TV and an Xbox."

"Kind of like Mole Town," Joe said. He turned to me. "What if Sal is behind this place too?"

It *was* like Mole Town. The decor was different, but the Secret City had a lot in common with the homeless camp we'd found under the train station. And it was Sal who had engineered the whole thing up there.

"It's hard to believe Sal would really be capable of all this," I said to Joe.

"Who?" Layla asked.

We didn't answer right away. If Layla really didn't know she had a long-lost homeless great-uncle who might also be a cult leader, I figured now probably wasn't the time to tell her.

"Do you have any idea who the Grandmaster might be?" I asked her instead.

"Nope. He's not around much, and when he is, he never takes off his mask," she said, pausing to think. "He does seem older than everyone else, though. At least I think it's a he. He never speaks, so it's hard to tell. He always just stands there with his big trident and has Keith speak for him."

Joe and I exchanged a look. So the Grandmaster was a brilliant treasure-obsessed engineer who never spoke? That was a pretty unique criminal profile, and I could think of only one person who fit it.

Layla's great-uncle Sal.

"It's got to be him," I said to Joe.

"What are you guys talking about?" Layla asked.

Joe hesitated. "I want to be able to trust you, Layla—I just don't know if I can."

"You have to believe me," she pleaded, grabbing hold of the bars like she was the one locked inside instead of us. "What can I do to convince you I'm telling the truth?"

"Do you think you could get us out of here?" I asked.

She fidgeted nervously before answering. "I don't know. But I'll try."

Then she reached through the bars and grabbed Joe's hand. "Thank you for coming to find me. It's the sweetest, bravest thing anyone has ever done for me."

"I, um, you're welcome" was all he managed to stammer before footsteps interrupted him.

"I have to go," Layla said, withdrawing her hand and quickly pushing the tray of food through the bars. "I'll do my best to come back for you."

Another Knight stepped around the corner. "They need us down at the altar. Keith says it's time."

Layla gave us a quick glance and hurried after the other Knight.

"Time for what?" I asked as they disappeared around the corner.

"I think we're about to find out," Joe said, pointing to the amphitheater below.

A dozen or so Knights in masks and robes gathered around the altar, where an object was draped in red cloth. Layla and the other guard ran up to join the rest of them as Keith raised his cane in the air.

"Behold, the Grandmaster approaches!"

FROM BEYOND THE GRAVE

14

JOE

WATCHED IN AMAZEMENT AS ANOTHER FIGURE approached the altar dressed in the same robe and mask as the rest. He carried a trident that looked just like the one in the Admiral's statue.

The Grandmaster walked to the top of the steps in front of the vault, lifted the trident, and banged the blunt end on the ground three times. The rest of the Knights folded their arms and bowed their heads.

The Grandmaster banged the trident on the ground three more times, and everyone lifted their heads to face him.

"Are you seeing this?" I whispered to Frank.

"It's like we've traveled back to the eighteenth century," he said in hushed awe. "We may be the first outsiders to witness something like this."

"Yeah, and it's freaking me out," I said.

Keith stepped forward and bowed to the Grandmaster, who banged his trident on the ground another two times. Keith turned to face the rest of the Knights.

"Our exalted and benevolent Grandmaster says that it is time to unlock the mysteries left to us and claim our inheritance. The Secret Order of the Knights of the Bay must again rise to the wealth and power that is our destiny!" he announced to wild cheers.

"Unveil the Key to the City of Fortune!"

Two Knights stepped forward and dramatically swept away the red cloth, revealing the giant bronze key that had once hung from the Admiral's statue. Keith lifted the key and carried it up the steps to the waiting Grandmaster, kneeling before him to present it.

The Grandmaster took the key from Keith and held it aloft to more cheers. Then he turned to the vault door.

"Here we go," I whispered, secretly excited to see if Sal was right about the pirate treasure.

The room went totally silent. The Grandmaster inserted the key into the giant keyhole. It fit perfectly.

The door swung open slowly on its own. The crowd inched forward to see what was inside.

The vault was cavernous—big enough to hold more treasure than anyone could imagine—only it was empty. The only thing in the center of the stone floor was a single sheet of paper.

Gasps and murmurs filled the room as it dawned on the Knights that their treasure—the one they'd given up their normal, aboveground lives for—wasn't there.

Keith rushed into the vault to pick up the sheet of parchment.

"It's from the Admiral," he said, earning more gasps from the Knights. He began to read aloud:

> "To those whose eyes have invaded this, the Temple's innermost sanctuary, without invitation, you have a choice. Choose wisely and be granted treasure, though perhaps not the kind you seek.
>
> Ever since my beloved wife passed away, leaving me with no heirs of my own, it has been my sincerest wish to leave my fortune to my brothers in the Knights. This was in order to carry on our sacred mission of bringing prosperity to Bayport. However, I have since discovered that greed has driven those same brothers to betray me. This is as crushing to me as the loss of a cherished family member. It is with heaviness in my soul that I choose to revoke my brothers' inheritance.
>
> My treasure now resides out of the reach of treacherous hands, close to my heart, and only my beloved and I hold the keys."

There were murmurs and angry grumblings.

"Hold on, there's more," Keith said, and continued reading:

"There is, however, another even more valuable treasure to be retained by the honest among you. Turn away from your greedy pursuits and you shall keep the greatest treasure: your own life. Should you still embark on stealing that which gleams and sparkles, do so at the peril of your own soul. For a curse is upon it, and should you seek it with impure intent, you shall only be rewarded with agony. After traveling to the world's darkest corners, my ships have returned with more than mere treasure. I have come to possess a dark magic so powerful that even my own death cannot stop it. Choose to defy me—and desecrate the Knights' legacy—and I shall own your soul. And that soul I shall destroy."

Keith paused and looked up. "It's signed, 'the Last Knight, Admiral James T. Bryant.'"

Shaking with rage, the Grandmaster tore the letter from Keith's hands and roared so loudly that the sound echoed off the walls.

The other Knights gasped. The Grandmaster had broken his silence.

It was something mute Sal never would have been able to

do. "Preposterous!" the Grandmaster bellowed in a distinctively deep, gravelly growl.

That voice didn't belong to Mr. Schneider, either. And it definitely wasn't Delia Hixson's. I knew that voice—this wasn't the first time I'd heard it say that word.

The Grandmaster was Zeke!

AT DAGGER POINT

15

FRANK

WE'D BEEN RIGHT ABOUT OUR CULPRIT being a tunnel-dwelling mole-man— we'd just picked the wrong mole. I knew it from the second the Grandmaster opened his gravelly mouth.

The really *preposterous* thing was how nice Zeke had seemed when he was giving us the lay of the land in Mole Town. I didn't like to be duped, but any thoughts of getting back at him would have to wait.

"Bring me the prisoner!" Zeke screamed.

I gulped. As far as I knew, my brother and I were the only prisoners around.

"Do you think he knows about the key we found in the Admiral?" I asked Joe.

He patted his pocket to make sure the key was still there. "I don't know, but after hearing that letter, I can pretty much guarantee he'd want to get ahold of it if he did."

"I say we make another run for it the second they open the gate," I told Joe.

Joe nodded. "It may be the only chance we get."

I was seriously contemplating swallowing the key like the Admiral had when two Knights dragged a raggedy-looking man in shackles to the altar.

Sal.

"Tell me where the treasure is!" Zeke yelled in Sal's face. Apparently he'd given up the whole silent shtick altogether.

Sal, on the other hand, hadn't. But for him it wasn't a shtick. No matter how much Zeke screamed and yelled, Sal wasn't going to answer. Because he couldn't.

"Tell me where it is now, you bum, or I'll show you what a real curse feels like!" Zeke stabbed the air with his trident.

Sal looked terrified but stood his ground.

Keith piped up, "Um, excuse me, Grandmaster, sir, but I don't think he can talk."

"Just because he can't talk doesn't mean he can't tell us what he knows." Zeke jabbed a gloved finger at Sal's chest. "You know where the Admiral hid that treasure, and you're going to write down exactly how to find it."

One of the Knights ran up with a notepad and a pen. Zeke grabbed it and thrust it into Sal's hands. "Now start writing."

Sal scribbled something and handed it to Keith. "He says he can't," Keith said. "That it's cursed."

"You really are crazy if you think a phony curse is going to stop us from claiming what's rightfully ours," Zeke bellowed. "Tell us where it is or I will throw you into that vault and seal it."

Sal looked absolutely petrified, but that didn't stop him from dropping the notepad on the ground and shaking his head vigorously. Zeke turned to Keith. "Throw him in a cell. He has exactly one hour to write us a story, and if it doesn't have a happy ending, into the vault he goes."

Sal struggled as Keith and Scott dragged him away, only to reappear minutes later as they threw him into the cell next to ours.

Joe and I rushed to the gated window between the cells as soon as the Knights left.

"Are you okay?" I asked.

Sal was so startled he just about jumped out of his boots. It took him a second to realize the four eyes peering at him through the little window belonged to a couple of regular dudes and not ghosts.

Sal scribbled a note.

Who are you? How did you get here?

"Frank and Joe Hardy," I said. "The underworld's best teenage detectives."

He thought about it for a second and then scribbled another note.

If you're such great detectives, why are you locked down here?

"He has a point," Joe said.

No one is supposed to know about the Secret City, he wrote. *How'd you find it?*

It had been one of the most eventful days in the history of eventful days and we didn't have time to explain it all, so I did my best to give him the short version.

After we had caught him up on the basics, Joe finished with, "So, um, we actually kind of thought the bad guy might be you."

"Sorry about that," I said sheepishly. "But it's been Zeke the entire time! He's the Grandmaster."

Sal looked baffled as he scrawled another note.

Zeke? What does he have to do with it? And why is the Admiral's ghost trying to steal its own treasure? It's supposed to be guarding the treasure from thieves.

"Ghost?" Joe repeated.

"He must think Zeke and his gang are the treasure-guarding ghosts from the story Curly told us," I whispered to Joe. I turned back to Sal. "Those aren't ghosts. It's just Zeke and a bunch of people who think they're descendants of Admiral Bryant's secret society."

Sal thought for a moment before replying.

I thought the Admiral's ghost sounded familiar. But I traced the forebears myself. He's not related to any of the original Knights. Sal held up the paper, mouthing the words *I don't understand.*

"We were hoping you could explain it to us," I said. "We know you'd been obsessed with finding the treasure before you lost your, uh, before your accident, and we know you told your niece that Layla was taken here."

Sal wrote quickly, his hand flying across the page.

I was sure only I knew about the Secret City. When I saw the Knights carrying away Layla last week, I thought the Admiral had sent his ghosts to take revenge on me for opening the vault.

"So you really have been in there?" Joe asked.

Sal took a deep breath, closed his eyes, and nodded yes.

"But how did you get it open without the key?" I asked.

I planned to steal the key from the statue, but I was able to safe-crack the lock on my own, so I didn't have to.

"Did you take the treasure?" Joe blurted.

No! Sal wrote with such force that the pen tore the paper. *The vault was empty. I read the Admiral's note, and I knew the curse was real!*

Sal had been writing fast before, but he really picked up the pace now.

I knew then that my obsession with the treasure was what caused me to be struck mute. It was a warning! Like a fool I ignored it. I knew from journals I'd found that Grandmasters took vows of silence to protect their identities underground. It was how they managed to go unnoticed. I should have known my own silence wasn't a coincidence.

Sal tore off the page for us to read and resumed writing.

But my greed also blinded me to the truth. For years I searched for the treasure—decades researching and planning. I burned every bit of it that night—my notes, blueprints of the tunnels, even the genealogy proving my family's inheritance. It wasn't ours to inherit. My ancestor betrayed the Admiral over two hundred years ago, and now I'd done the same. But the Admiral was right. There was still a treasure left for me to claim. My life.

Joe and I were riveted by the page in front of us as Sal continued to write.

The Admiral had given me a choice and I took it. I thought the curse was over. I put all my energy into making the old train depot a real home for those with nowhere left to go. But then ghosts started to appear in the tunnels. And when they took Layla, I knew the curse wasn't over.

Sal tore off another sheet and handed it to us.

I saw them carry her into the tunnels. But I was too afraid to follow. I tried to tell my niece—even wrote her a note saying so—but she didn't believe me. Even if Layla doesn't know who I am, she's still family. I couldn't let her be punished for my sins. So I did something I swore I'd never do again. I came back to the Secret City to save her. But I failed. And now they want me to betray the Admiral all over again!

Sal was shaking by the time he finished writing his story.

"Do you know where the treasure is?" I asked gently.

Sal shook his head violently.

It's not meant to be found, he wrote. *Even if I knew, I would never say.*

"Well, if you don't tell Zeke something," Joe said, "it's

going to end badly for all of us. We can't rescue Layla if we're sealed in a stone vault."

"I'm not so sure I'm the one who needs rescuing," a voice said softly.

"Layla!" Joe cried.

There she was, still wearing her mask and standing outside the cell with a set of keys dangling from her finger. She'd come back for us . . . just like she'd promised.

"We don't have much time," she said, sliding a key into the cell door. "Everyone else is searching for the treasure. I was able to get the keys, but they could be back any minute."

The cell door swung open and Layla unlocked our shackles. Joe grabbed Layla's hand. "I knew you were one of the good guys!"

"Thanks, Layla!" I said, taking the keys and unlocking Sal's cell and shackles.

Sal ran out, wrapped her in a big hug, and started to cry.

"Um, who's this?" she asked.

"Layla, meet your great-uncle Sal," I said.

I could practically see her confusion through the mask.

"We'll explain later. Come on!" Joe grabbed her hand and ran toward the stone steps that led down to the amphitheater.

As soon as we reached the bottom, we were surrounded.

"Grab the old man and the girl!" Zeke yelled.

Joe jumped in front of Layla and I moved to defend Sal, tackling one of the Knights to the floor.

As I rolled back to my feet, I saw Zeke throw down his

trident and try to grab Layla while Joe was busy tussling with Keith. Before I could run toward her, Zeke pulled a long dagger from his robe and held the point to her neck.

"Anybody else tries anything and the lady here gets it," he said.

"Let her go or you really will need a mask when I'm done with you," threatened Joe, scrambling to his feet.

Zeke ignored him. "There's only one way you're going to save your long-lost niece, Sally boy. Pick up that notepad and write down exactly where the treasure is."

Sal shook his head back and forth and wrote, *Cursed*.

"You really think I'm going to let some superstition stop me from reclaiming my rightful place in the world? Now start writing!"

Sal shook his head even harder.

"If you don't"—Zeke yanked off Layla's mask and pressed the tip of the dagger to her cheek—"she joins the rest of the ghosts down here."

Sal's lips began to tremble as he bent down to pick up the notepad. He looked at Layla for a long, agonizing moment before scribbling something. I strained to see what he was writing, but Zeke yelled, "Get back!"

Zeke ripped the pad out of Sal's hands the second his pen stopped moving. He didn't let go of Layla, but he did let the knife slip to his side as he looked at what Sal had written.

Zeke's trident was lying close enough that I could reach the blunt end of it with my foot. I made eye contact with

Joe and kicked the end of the trident as squarely as I could, sending it sliding across the stone floor.

My aim was right on, but I'd miscalculated how much force I'd need to get it to Joe. I kicked it hard enough that it hit a bump and started to catch air. Joe was ready for it, though. He slammed his foot down on the blunt end just as the trident sailed past, causing the forked end to fly upward, skewering Zeke right in his red-robed rump.

Zeke yowled and let go of Layla. Joe dove for her, shoving her out of harm's way. I leaped toward Zeke before he could make a run for it, but one of his henchmen blocked me, knocking me to the ground. A bunch of the Knights turned tail, but there were still five or six ready to defend their Grandmaster, which meant we had our hands full fending off a gang of masked fanatics.

Meanwhile, the Grandmaster had turned and fled.

DOWN THE DRAIN

DRAIN

16

JOE

LAYLA SMACKED ONE OF THE KNIGHTS with her mask and then pulled his robe over his head so he couldn't see. Frank had another Knight in an arm bar, and Sal was sparring with yet another. The four of us were doing a good job holding them off, but every second we were fighting meant that Zeke was getting farther away.

Frank realized it too. He grabbed the trident and started swinging it around in a circle, forcing the Knights to back out of reach. He was doing more than just defending himself, though; he was herding them away from Layla and me.

"You and Layla go after Zeke," he yelled. "Sal and I can hold them off!"

"Thanks!" I yelled back, grabbing Layla by the hand and running toward the tunnel where Zeke had fled.

I recognized the torch-lit tunnel as the same one Frank and I had been led down when we were captured. Zeke wasn't in sight. I'd hoped we'd spot him in one of the other three tunnels when we reached the crossroads, but we had no such luck. One of the tunnels was pitch-black, one curved out of view, and the other was only partially lit before it receded into darkness.

"Any idea which way he might have gone?" I asked Layla.

"No, it's like a maze down here. Besides, they told me a lot of the tunnels were booby-trapped," she said.

I cringed as I recalled my close call on the rock wall. Who knew what kind of nasty surprises might await us if we chose wrong?

"One out of three aren't great odds, but we may have to wing it," I said, getting ready to start down the curved tunnel.

"Hey, is that torch moving on its own?" Layla said, pointing down the partially lit tunnel.

I had to strain my eyes, but she was right. Way down the third tunnel, a speck of light was bobbing up and down.

"That's not a torch, it's a flashlight. It has to be him!" I said, and took off running with Layla right behind me.

We were gaining on him, but by the time we reached the place where the torches went out, the light had vanished. Layla and I each grabbed a torch and kept running.

We spotted Zeke's light at the next intersection. It

disappeared again a moment later, only this time we saw it veer to the right. We were close enough now to make out Zeke's shadow when the light went out altogether. We sprinted toward the spot where we'd last seen it, but there was nothing there.

"Where did he go?" Layla asked, looking around. "He couldn't have just vanished."

"Maybe he saw us following him and nixed the light," I said, walking farther down the tunnel. I had just started to notice the air getting draftier when my torch made a strange sizzling sound.

Then, *plunk!* A drop of water landed on my head. It occurred to me that the one place I hadn't thought to look was up.

There was another tunnel directly above me. It was just wide enough for one person to climb the iron rungs that were bolted into the stone. Water dripped down the walls from somewhere above, which meant we couldn't be too far from the surface. I had no idea how high the ladder went, but I could see Zeke's silhouette rising behind his flashlight, so following him wouldn't be a problem. At least not until he reached the top.

"I think I found him," I said. "Are you up for a climb?"

"Let's go get him," Layla replied.

"We can't climb and hold torches at the same time," I said, "so we're going to have to go by touch—and the ladder's a bit slick. It could be dangerous."

"Dangerous for you, maybe," she said, throwing down her torch and pulling herself up effortlessly. "But after ten years of gymnastics, this will be a cinch for me."

The ladder was no joke. I started to wonder if we'd ever reach the top. The dripping water was getting worse the higher we climbed, making the situation even hairier.

"His light went out!" Layla said as the tunnel plunged into darkness. "Do you think that means he reached the top?"

"I sure hope so," I said, trying not to think about just how far we had to drop if he managed to kick us off. "Be on guard."

"Don't worry, I went first so you could break my fall," she said.

I laughed. It was the same kind of joke I would have made to Frank.

"Ow!" she grunted. "Either I just reached the top or the air above me got really hard."

"If it's a hatch, it should either lift or slide. Is there a handle?"

"I don't feel any . . . wait . . . got it!" she said as the hatch slid open. Cold water splashed down on top of us, almost causing me to lose my grip.

"There he is!" Layla lifted herself out of the tunnel and took off running.

I climbed up after her into an old, wet drainage tunnel. Zeke's flashlight illuminated the tunnel not far ahead, where he had stopped and was trying to pry loose a metal gate blocking another hatch in the ceiling above him. He'd ditched his mask, and he was close enough that I could read the panic on his face when he saw us coming.

"I think this is part of Bayport's original sewer system," I called out to Layla, catching up to her. "We must be close to the surface."

"Good. We won't have far to drag him after I knock him out," she said.

By the time Zeke finally managed to yank the grate off the hatch opening, we were only a few yards away, too close for him to make a break for it. Instead he whipped out his dagger and thrust it in our direction.

"That's close enough!" he shouted as Layla and I skidded to a stop just out of reach of the blade's tip.

I looked around for something to use as a weapon, but all I saw was a metal ring embedded in the wall above me. I knew from Urbex that sewer workers held on to them when the water rose. There was no way I was getting that thing free, so I was forced to use the next best thing: a bluff.

"You might as well just give up," I told him. "You can't reach for the ladder without dropping your weapon, and we're close enough to grab you the second you do."

"You're also close enough to get cozy with my dagger if you take another step," he added, jabbing the knife forward.

"I guess it's a standoff, then," I said, lowering myself into a defensive crouch.

Zeke's dagger sliced through the air. "Not if I just turn the two of you into rat food."

"You're in a lot of trouble, Zeke, but no one's been hurt yet. I don't think you want to add murder to your list of crimes."

"You're right, I don't," he said. "But I'm too close to finding the treasure to let a couple of kids stop me from fulfilling my destiny."

"But according to Sal, you're not even related to any of the Knights!"

"So what!" he snapped. "Without me the Knights wouldn't exist anymore. I'm the one who resurrected them! I'm the one who will reclaim the wealth and power that are rightfully ours."

"The only thing that's rightfully yours is a jail cell!" Layla sneered.

"The treasure is mine!" he yelled. "I wasn't supposed to be a bum. My father was a wealthy businessman. His fortune was my birthright, and it was taken from me by Sal's parents. They bought my father's company out from under him when he fell ill and cheated me out of my inheritance!"

So that was the link between Zeke and Sal! He stabbed the air with his dagger. "It's only fair that I get the treasure that was meant for Sal's family. I'm claiming it as justice for what was taken from me!"

Zeke was on the verge of flying out of control.

"It sounds like you got a raw deal," I said, trying to

sympathize with him so he'd calm down. "I'd be mad too, but there are other ways to make things right."

"Don't you think I tried?" he hissed. "The system is rigged against people like me. Sal's parents were powerful people in Bayport. I lost every penny I had trying to fight them."

Zeke's gravelly voice came out sounding like a wild animal's growl.

"They put me out on the street, but that wasn't even enough for them. The police issued a warrant for my arrest because they claimed I was harassing Sal's family. They drove me underground like . . . like a *mole*."

Zeke was seething, and I could tell from that last comment that his anger had settled on me.

"I didn't mean to offend you when I called the underground dwellers mole people," I said. "The town under the station is awesome. It seems like you and your friends have a good home there."

"I'm not like them," Zeke spat back. "None of those people have an ounce of ambition, and half of them are just plain crazy."

He smiled. "But Sal. Sure, he was off his rocker, but there was something different about him. I didn't know who his parents were when he first started showing up underground; I was just drawn to how determined he seemed. Like he was on a mission. I made it my business to get to know him better."

"Sal didn't tell you about the treasure! He was shocked you even knew about it," I said, hoping to keep him talking.

"Oh, there are ways to get to know a person without talking to them."

"You followed him to the Secret City?" Layla asked eagerly.

"Not without getting lost or stumbling into a trap, you didn't," I cut in. "It would have been impossible for you to find it on your own, and Sal said he burned all his plans and blueprints."

"I found out about the Secret City long before Sal burned those documents." Zeke laughed meanly. "Once I realized who he was, I was determined to figure out what he was up to. The way he was always looking over his shoulder and carrying strange bundles made it obvious he was hiding something. He would vanish for days, giving me plenty of time to locate those documents in his train car and copy them."

Zeke shook his head. "At first I thought the whole thing was just a bunch of make-believe. I almost threw away all the copies I'd made, but something told me not to. Good thing I didn't. One of those papers was a map that led me right to the Secret City, and once I saw the vault with my own eyes, I knew the treasure was real."

"So you stole Sal's plans?" I accused.

"I didn't steal them," he growled, "I implemented them! At first I just meant to take the treasure for myself, but I needed help to carry out his plans properly. And I realized that using the treasure to rally a new order of Knights was my chance to take back everything that had ever been stolen from me. With patience and careful planning, I could rule the entire town . . . just like the Admiral!"

Zeke was getting caught up in his own story, gesturing wildly and punching the air with his dagger for emphasis.

"Every king needs subjects," he said. "So I re-formed the Knights with the descendants of its original members and became their Grandmaster. Some of my followers were skeptical at first, but once they saw the Secret City they became believers."

Layla cleared her throat and raised her hand. "Hello, nonbeliever here."

"You would have believed once you saw the treasure," Zeke said, disappointment creeping into his voice. "You could have helped make right what your family did to me."

I could see the confusion on Layla's face, but there wasn't time to explain.

"You can't blame Sal's whole family for what his parents did years ago," I shouted at Zeke.

"I gave her a chance," he sneered before turning to Layla. "But I can't trust you anymore. Which means you don't leave me any choice."

Zeke raised the dagger and began to splash toward us through the tunnel.

Either I figured out a way to keep him talking, or we were going to be getting a closer look at that dagger. "You still haven't told us what Sal wrote on that piece of paper earlier," I said, hoping he'd take the bait.

"I'm not sure it would be in my best interest to tell you that. Not that it would do you much good anyway," Zeke said, brandishing the dagger. "I have a treasure to retrieve. I just thought it was important that you understand why I'm doing what I'm doing. Not just for me, but for Bayport. Sometimes unpleasant sacrifices are necessary evils on the path to greatness."

We'd gotten our confession, but I could tell Zeke never doubted for a second that he'd still get away with it. He wasn't the only one who knew his way around a tunnel, though, and I was willing to bet that he didn't have any Urbex training under his belt.

While Zeke had been talking, the water in the drainpipe had started inching its way to our ankles. That meant it was probably raining aboveground, and one of the first things all urban explorers learn is, "When it rains, no drains!"

Zeke narrowed his eyes and lunged at us with the dagger.

Layla grabbed on to me. And I grabbed on to the metal ring on the wall. Zeke, who had his back to the rumbling sound that suddenly erupted from the tunnel, didn't grab anything. The rumble turned into a roar as an angry wall of water burst out of the darkness.

"Flash flood!" I cried.

By the time Zeke turned around, it was too late. The wave crashed into us with the force of a tsunami and carried him away screaming.

Which was kind of inconvenient, considering he still

hadn't gotten around to telling us where the treasure was.

I held on to the ring with all my strength as the wave carried Zeke past us.

"Hold on!" I yelled to Layla.

"I was gonna tell you the same thing!" she yelled back.

The water started to slow to a steady rush. It hadn't stopped rising, though; it was already past our waists and steadily growing higher.

"We're going to have to swim for it!" I screamed.

"Ready when you are!" she yelled.

I'm a good swimmer, but the current was so strong that it took everything I had to get to the hatch in the sewer's ceiling. I grabbed on to the bottom rung of the ladder with one hand and reached behind me for Layla with the other. Together we swam to safety through the open hatch.

Okay, maybe "safety" wasn't the right word. We'd made it through the hatch into the portal above, but the portal was sealed! The door above it was locked tight, trapping us inside with the water rising second by second. The water surged higher and higher until there were only a couple feet of air left.

"I don't want to drown, Joe," Layla pleaded as the water inched past our necks.

ZOMBIE GRAVEYARD
17

FRANK

SAL HAD BEEN SMART ENOUGH TO CLEAR out of the way before I started swinging the trident around me in a circle. I felt like samurai master Miyamoto Musashi in *The Book of Five Rings*, sending the rest of the Knights diving out of the way while Joe and Layla made their escape.

By the time I stopped spinning, I was dizzy enough to fall over. Sal didn't miss a beat, though. He ran past the dazed Knights, grabbed me by the arm, and dragged me through a hidden exit behind the vault. A few twists and turns later, we stepped out into a dark, rainy alley. By now, I had a pretty good guess as to where the treasure was. The Admiral's letter in the vault had said the only other person who knew where the treasure was hidden was his wife. Seeing as she was already dead when he wrote the note, I knew exactly where to find her.

"Come on, Sal, let's make for the Admiral's Tomb," I said.

Sal shook his head so hard I thought he might give himself whiplash.

"I know you're worried about ghosts, but there's no scientific evidence that they actually exist," I explained.

Sal shook his head no again. He took out the soggy pad of paper and wrote two words before the ink smeared: *The Curse.*

I tried a different tactic.

"The Admiral said the curse was for people seeking the treasure, right? But we're not even doing that. We're trying to save Layla and Joe. The Admiral would have done the same."

Sal nodded slowly and took his first step in the direction of the graveyard, a look of grim determination on his face.

I gave him a reassuring pat on the back. "Layla is lucky to have you as a great-uncle, Sal. I think the Admiral would approve."

The corner of Sal's mouth turned up just a little.

I made a quick stop on the way, ducking into a convenience store to grab Sal a fresh notepad and use the phone before we reached the cemetery's ancient black gates.

The cemetery was the oldest—and spookiest—in Bayport, filled with three-hundred-year-old graves, raised marble mausoleums, and strange statues. The Admiral's Tomb was the cemetery's most famous mausoleum, which is a monument that houses the chamber where the actual corpse is, usually in some kind of stone sarcophagus.

The tomb had large marble columns that framed a giant slab of a door engraved with an Eye of Providence—like the one over the Secret City vault, only bigger and more piercing. I'd shrugged off Sal's fears, but the place was bone-chilling!

We had almost reached it when Sal came to an abrupt stop and took off running like he'd seen a ghost. Only it wasn't a ghost. Not technically, at least.

I stood there gaping as the door to the Admiral's Tomb creaked open, and pair of gore-drenched zombies came stumbling out!

TOMB RAIDERS 18

JOE

THE HATCH DOOR WOULDN'T BUDGE no matter how hard I pushed and pounded. At the rate the water was rising, Layla and I had only a minute tops before we were entirely submerged. Then I realized why I couldn't get it open. I was supposed to pull instead of push! There was just enough of a groove in the metal for me to hook my fingers into and yank. It flew open, dumping a few hundred years' worth of dirt onto our heads in the process.

I managed to drag myself out, pull Layla up after me, and slam the hatch door before it could overflow. "Are you okay?" I asked, panting.

"Thanks to you I am," she said breathlessly. "I didn't

think we were going to make it out in time." She looked around. "Where are we anyway?"

That was a good question. There was just enough light to make out shapes and shadows. Which meant that wherever we were, it was either on the surface or close to it.

We were in a large room with high ceilings and creepy statues lurking in the corners. There were also more cobwebs than I wanted to think about and a platform that held a pair of long, rectangular boxes.

I started to get a sinking feeling. The boxes looked just about the right size to be . . .

"Uh, Joe, are those coffins?" Layla asked with a quiver in her voice.

"I think I know where we are," I said as the pieces started to click into place.

"We're in some kind of tomb, aren't we?"

"Yeah. I wonder if it's the Admiral's."

"Is this where the treasure is hidden?" she asked.

"It would make sense," I replied. "The letter said the treasure was out of reach, where only the Admiral and his wife could get it. And his wife has been in here the whole time."

"You don't think this place has a light switch, do you?" Layla joked, picking up a tall candelabra that held three ancient, mostly melted candles. "I left my fire-making spell back at Hogwarts, and this place is giving me the willies."

"I don't know about a light switch, but maybe this will help," I said, pulling the emergency kit from my pocket. I had totally forgotten about it until Layla spotted the candles. I just hoped the kit's plastic case had kept the water out.

I removed a match, scraped it against the wall, and—bingo!—it lit on the first try. The old wicks on the candelabra sparked and fizzed stubbornly, but they lit too.

"And let there be light!" I announced as the tomb became visible. Thick cobwebs covered just about everything, and there was so much dust floating around that the air itself seemed to shimmer in the candlelight. And those statues I'd spotted? Gargoyles with mouthless, bird-beaked faces . . . just like the ones on the Knights' masks.

"I think this place may have been less creepy in the dark," Layla muttered. She turned to me and started laughing. "You look ridiculous!"

"I, what . . . ?" And then I laughed too. We were both covered with so much muck from our crawl through the hatch that we barely looked human.

I tried not to shudder as I pushed aside a curtain of cobwebs on my way toward the giant slab of marble that I figured must be the tomb door.

I paused for a last look at the coffins.

"Rest in peace, guys," I said.

I was about to turn back toward the door when something caught my eye. The his-and-hers coffins were decorated with strange markings. One had a big trident and that creepy eye symbol, which had to be the Admiral's, and the other had an angel, which I figured was his wife's.

Hers also had an intricate design carved into the top. I crept closer and I realized there was something hidden in the center of it: a keyhole. And it looked like it would fit the key the Admiral had swallowed before he died.

I tried to remember what his letter had said. Something about the treasure being close to his heart in a place only he and his wife knew about. "Layla, do you remember exactly what the Admiral's letter said? The last part about him and his wife having the key to the treasure?"

"Sure. I thought it was kind of sweet, actually. He said, 'My treasure now resides out of the reach of treacherous hands, close to my heart, and only my beloved and I hold the keys,'" Layla recited.

I pulled the bandanna-wrapped key from my pocket. "I wonder if this is the key he was talking about." There was no way the detective in me was going to let me leave after finding the keyhole that might unlock the entire mystery.

"Um, Joe, what are you doing?" Layla asked as I started to creep toward the coffin.

"Just one second," I said absently. "I want to see something."

I took a deep breath, steadied myself, and inserted the key into the keyhole. It fit perfectly.

"I don't think this is such a good idea," Layla said.

She was right. It probably wasn't.

But I turned the key anyway.

There was a faint metallic click. I held my breath.

A little hidden compartment popped open. Candlelight flickered over something inside, only it wasn't treasure.

It was yet another, even smaller, bronze key.

NIGHT OF THE LIVING BRO

19

FRANK

FROZEN IN FEAR, I RACKED MY BRAIN for a rational explanation for the two monstrous creatures that had just pushed their way out of the Admiral's Tomb. That's when one of the zombies started yelling my name.

It was Joe and Layla! They were a mess, but they were very much alive.

"Frank!" Joe shouted, looking more human by the second as the rain rinsed off the mud that covered him.

"For a second there I was sure you were a couple of zombies!" I shouted back.

"Nope, we're very much un-undead, although I'm not sure we smell like it," he said, cringing as he took a sniff.

"Where's Zeke?" I asked. "Did he get away?"

"Well, more like swept away. Kind of like a goldfish flushed down the toilet of life," Joe said cryptically.

I was trying to figure out what that meant when Sal crept out from his hiding place behind a tombstone.

"Hey, Sal! They made it! They're not zombies at all!" I said, happy to see him.

"Um, guys, you were going to explain what you meant before when you said he was my uncle," Layla reminded us.

"Oh, uh, well . . ." I could tell Joe was fumbling for the right way to break it to her that she had a secret uncle her mom had neglected to tell her about.

"Maybe we should let Sal explain," I suggested. "Would that be okay, Sal?"

Sal nodded and pulled out the fresh notepad I'd picked up at the convenience store.

We gave Layla and her newly discovered uncle a little privacy to get acquainted, while Joe filled me in on the soggy showdown with Zeke. He also told me how he'd used the key we'd found in the Admiral's stomach to unlock a third key hidden in a secret compartment in Mrs. Bryant's coffin.

"No wonder the Admiral thought the key we found was important enough to swallow before he died," I said. "He and his dead wife actually had both keys! And without his key, a would-be thief wouldn't be able to retrieve his wife's key, so that must mean you need both keys before you can unlock the treasure."

"All three keys, actually," Joe said. "Because you need the

giant key from the statue to unlock the vault to even discover you need the other keys. This guy must have been really paranoid about security."

"Well, someone did kill him over it," I reminded Joe.

"So what's next, another key?"

"I don't think there is one," I said as it began to hit me just how clever the Admiral had been. "I think the key you found in the tomb is the key to the treasure."

"Okay, but we can't unlock a vault we can't find."

"I think the Admiral gave us everything we need to solve the mystery in his letter," I told Joe. "The Admiral wrote, 'My treasure now resides out of the reach of treacherous hands, close to my heart, and only my beloved and I hold the keys.' The part about the keys is literal, but the rest of it's a riddle. He's telling us exactly where the treasure is!"

"Um, he is?" Joe asked.

"Yup. Think about it. He said it's out of reach and close to his heart. There's only one place that meets both those criteria, and I have a good hunch exactly where that is."

Joe leaned forward in anticipation.

"It's in—" I began.

"HARDYS!" an angry voice bellowed. Sirens pierced the air as Chief Olaf came huffing toward us.

"Welcome back, Chief!" Joe said cheerfully as he slid the key back into his pocket. "Did you have a nice vacation?"

"Don't you 'nice vacation' me. I leave town for a few days and the whole place falls apart. Literally!" the chief muttered.

"I should have figured you two were caught up in the middle of this. Now, do you want to tell me why I'm getting calls from a high school newspaper telling me the Hardy boys need backup at the cemetery? Because if this is some kind of prank, I'm going to toss you in jail so fast your spinning will alter the rotation of the earth's axis."

"Nice analogy, Chief, although your science is a little off," I said, unable to help myself. "But it's no prank," I added quickly.

On the way to the cemetery, I'd used the phone at the convenience store to leave a message for Charlene, telling her to have the cops meet us at the Admiral's Tomb.

Charlene marched up right on cue, notepad in one hand and digital recorder in the other.

"Hi, Charlene," I said.

"You want to tell me what this is all about, Hardy?" Charlene and Chief Olaf said at the exact same time. "Well—" I began, when Charlene cut me off.

"Is that Layla? What's she doing with the silent homeless guy?" she asked as Layla walked up with Sal.

"Hi, Chief," Layla said.

"Layla? But—what—where—" the Chief fumbled. "Are you okay?"

"I'm fine," she said. "Thanks to Sal and Joe and Frank I am, anyway."

"Sal?" the Chief asked with a dumbfounded expression. "What does he have to do with—?"

"Dad!" Layla yelled, cutting him off as Deputy Hixson sprinted around the corner and swept her up in a huge hug.

"Baby girl, you have no idea how good it is to see you."

Joe put his arm around my shoulder. "Nothing like family, huh, bro?"

I didn't have to say anything. My brother already knew I was thinking the exact same thing.

"What about Daniel?" Deputy Hixson said as he pulled away from Layla. I explained that Daniel was safe and quickly described where he was in the Secret City. Deputy Hixson dispatched a crew of officers to rescue him.

"You're in real trouble, Hardys," the chief said from behind us. "I'd toss you in a cell right now for interfering with a police investigation if I didn't need you to tell me what the heck is going on here first."

"Excuse me, Chief," Deputy Hixson said, walking over to us with Layla and Sal on either side. "You're right, the boys have some explaining to do, but the important thing is that everyone is safe." The deputy pulled Layla close to him. "These three have been through a lot today. I think we can let Joe and Frank off the hook just this once. I have a feeling we'll have plenty of other chances to yell at them in the future," he said with a wink in our direction. "What do you say, Chief?"

"I think I need another vacation, is what I say," the chief said, getting a laugh out of everyone whether he meant to or not. "Fine, Deputy. I left you in charge, so it's your call."

"Yes!" Joe and I said at the same time, throwing each other a high five.

"But!" the chief barked, interrupting our celebration. "I want a full debriefing right this instant."

I was probably pressing my luck with the chief, but with the deputy on our side, I took my chances. I said we'd tell him everything . . . just as long as Charlene could sit in on it too.

Charlene eagerly agreed and jotted something down on her notepad, which she casually tilted in my direction so only I could see it.

Hardy—Ur the best.

Just then, I felt like it too.

Joe, Layla, and I brought everyone up to speed on everything: from Sal's discovery of the Secret City, to our discovery of Zeke's discovery of Sal's discovery, to Zeke's resurrection of the Admiral's secret society and the empty vault, to Zeke washing away in the tunnel beneath the Admiral's Tomb.

Okay, so there may have been a detail or two we "forgot" to mention.

Like the fact that the treasure wasn't just lost to history. And that we had a pretty good idea where it was.

THE FINAL RESTING PLACE

20

JOE

THE ONLY THING FRANK AND I HAD left to figure out was, what about the treasure?

"The detective in me wants to at least see if it's there," I said to my brother from across the booth. We had decided to reward ourselves with a post-case dinner at the Meet Locker, where we were wolfing down fries and milk shakes. My brother had just finished explaining his theory as to where the treasure was hidden.

"I'm with you," Frank agreed.

"But I can't help thinking about the Admiral's curse. I know, I know . . . ," I said before he could interject. "There's no scientific basis for the existence of curses, but so far everyone who's gone looking for the treasure has ended up dead, mute, crazy, or washed down a giant drain."

"The whole curse thing is superstitious nonsense, but . . ." Frank let his sentence trail off.

"But . . . ," I encouraged him.

"Well, after all the weird stuff that's happened, maybe we shouldn't take the chance, you know, just in case there's some stuff science hasn't quite figured out yet."

"Sounds good to me, dude. If someone is going to steal the Admiral's treasure, it isn't going to be the Hardy boys," I said.

"So it's settled," Frank declared, dipping a fry into his shake. "We'll sneak back to the Admiral's Tomb and return the keys so they can be buried with him and his wife like he originally wanted."

It was a good plan. Only . . .

"It would be a shame, though, not to at least take a peek first. I mean, just to see if your theory about where he stashed the treasure is right," I hedged.

Frank thought about it. "We wouldn't actually be trying to steal it as long as we didn't take anything, so technically the curse . . ."

"Which you don't believe in anyway," I reminded him.

"Right. The curse that doesn't exist anyway wouldn't apply to us. Our intent wouldn't be impure at all," Frank said, warming up to the idea of just a little bit more investigative mischief. "In a way, we'd kind of be honoring the Admiral, really."

"To the Admiral!" I said, raising my shake in tribute.

We waited until everyone was asleep to sneak out of our house and put Frank's theory to the test.

A bolt of excitement shot through me when Frank told me where he thought the treasure was hidden. We were headed back to the place where the whole adventure started.

The sinkhole.

Using headlamps and climbing ropes I'd borrowed from the Urbex group, we rappelled down into the pit that held the Admiral's sunken statue.

"Let's do it, dude," I said, grabbing hold of a notch in the Admiral's bronze sleeve and pulling myself up the statue's side. It's a good thing it had landed on its back, otherwise our destination would have been totally out of reach.

The giant book clutched to the Admiral's chest was even bigger up close and personal. Looking up at it from the ground, you never would have noticed the tiny keyhole hidden on its clasp.

And just as Frank had suspected, the key I'd found in Mrs. Bryant's coffin fit into it perfectly. The Admiral's letter had said the treasure was close to his heart, after all.

I made eye contact with Frank before turning the key. The book's cover popped open. Golden light reflected onto our faces from the hidden chamber within as we stared in silence before turning to each other with big grins.

Then we closed the book's cover, locked it tight, and crept back to the cemetery to return the key.

Admiral James T. Bryant really did have a heart of gold.

CHRISTOPHER ROWE, apprentice to Master Benedict Blackthorn, has learned to solve complex codes and puzzles. He can create powerful medicines, potions, and weapons . . . with maybe an unexpected explosion or two along the way. But when a mysterious cult begins to prey on London's apothecaries, the trail of murders grows closer and closer to Blackthorn's shop. Can Christopher discover the key to their terrible secret before his world is torn apart?

"MAGIC, ADVENTURE, AND THINGS THAT GO BOOM—I LOVE THIS BOOK."
—EOIN COLFER, author of the bestselling Artemis Fowl series

THE BLACKTHORN KEY

KEVIN SANDS

EBOOK EDITION ALSO AVAILABLE